WIND, WATER AND WINE

KASSIE ANDERS

A catalogue record for this book is available from the National Library of Australia.

National Library of Australia Cataloguing-in-Publication entry

Author: Kassie Anders

Title: **Wind, Water and Wine**

ISBN: (Print) 978-1-7642912-0-0

ISBN: (ePub) 978-1-7642912-1-7

ISBN: (Audiobook) 978-1-7642912-2-4

For my co-Canberrans

A note for my American readers. This book is written in UK/Australian English. Many of the words will be spelled differently from what you're used to - realised, colour, centre, grey etc.

In addition, we do not share your fondness for the letter "Z." I realise you may find this difficult and offer my humble apologies. We make up for this by using a plethora of "L's" where you would make do with one. Marvellous.

No Generative AI was used on any part of this book. The words and artwork were all produced by human hand and always will be.

ACKNOWLEDGEMENT OF COUNTRY

This book is set on Ngunnawal land. Hayley Price Books acknowledges the Traditional Custodians of the ACT, the Ngunnawal people, and we pay our respects to Elders past, present and emerging. We acknowledge and respect their continuing culture and the contribution they make to the life of this city and this region.

Sovereignty of Ngunnawal land was never ceded. Always was, always will be Aboriginal land.

A NOTE ABOUT THE SETTING OF THIS BOOK

In the summer of 2019-2020, Australia suffered from catastrophic bushfires that stretched our emergency services to the limits. Homes were lost and, sadly, so were lives. In the east, southern New South Wales and the Central Coast were hammered by these fires.

In 2020, rain fell, and we heaved a collective sigh of relief. Thanks to the courage and dedication of the emergency services, many of them volunteers, we had survived a once-in-a-century event.

The rain fell and continued to fall for the next two years, and the country suffered again from horrendous floods on the back of the hideous fires we had just lived through.

Lake George lies in New South Wales, just north of the Australian Capital Territory (ACT), in which Canberra, the country's capital city, sits. The lake had been dry for twenty years until 2016, when heavy rains partly filled it. During dry spells, the lake is used to graze animals. It is not fed or drained by a river or the sea, lying completely inland.

The rains of 2020 to 2022 filled the lake more than many locals could recall, and the water that had been contained to a small area to the southeast reached almost to the Federal Highway in the west. This event forms the backdrop for this story.

A SMALLER NOTE ABOUT THE SETTING OF THIS BOOK

There is no Carson Street in Cook. I made it up to avoid hordes of tourists pouring through the little suburb's streets in search of Abi's house, like Lombard Street in San Francisco.

1

They say there's a first time for everything, and without a doubt, this was the first time I'd ever seen a naked woman come out of Lake Ginninderra. I'd sat on the bench at the northern end of Yerra beach with my coffee, and I'd taken no more than a couple of sips before she appeared, and I do mean appeared. I didn't see the water boil and splash as she swam through the shallows or anything like that. One second she wasn't there, the next, she was.

Belconnen, 23rd March 2022. Early autumn, not bitter cold yet, but not warm either. The leaves on the deciduous trees had begun their journey towards death, hints of brown and red around the edges. Soon they'd be a blaze of breathtaking colour, then they'd fall to the floor while the evergreens mocked the nakedness of the bare trees the leaves left behind.

In Canberra, there's an urban legend that says you aren't allowed to turn your heating on or wear your puffer jacket before Anzac Day—April 25th. Because I'm a great believer in tradition, I didn't have my puffer jacket on, but I did have a long, hooded top over my alpaca t-shirt. It was a sharp morning, and a small puff of air in front of my face accompanied every breath, but that may have been due to the coffee, I suppose. The new arrival, however, could not be considered appropriately dressed, unless her birthday suit met the requirements. Who knows these days?

I think I'd gone into mild shock at the sight of her, which might explain why I sat there and stared, open-mouthed, as she walked towards me, long, blonde hair plastered to her head and down past her shoulders. She didn't have a bad figure. Wait a second. Who am I kidding? I'd die for that figure, damn it. She might have been around twenty-five, but I've never been very good with ages, and the nakedness served as a distraction, so I'll give myself some slack on my guess. Water flowed from long, slender fingers and drew a pair of wet lines in the sand somebody had trucked in to build the beaches around the man-made lake.

I shook myself, and my inner woman returned from wherever she had run off to when the naked supermodel showed up. She might not have been a supermodel, but she did have the looks and the figure. I muttered a quiet blasphemy at myself, shook my head, and hurried towards her. "Are you all right?"

She stopped and stared at me, as though she had only just noticed me. I was no glamour girl, and my clothes weren't eye-catching, just old track pants and my Mambo hoodie. She might have noticed me sooner if I'd been wearing something trendy like White Fox, but these days, I didn't spend much money on clothes. I never had, in fact. If I had ever been down with the hip crew, those days lay long behind me. She stared at me as though I'd just stepped out of a spaceship, then she answered. "All right." Not the most effusive of replies, and not exactly the most reassuring response, given she'd just come out of the lake naked, but at least she'd answered. True blue Aussie accent, too.

When I reached her, I tugged my hoodie over my head and handed it to her. "Put this on, kiddo. You must be freezing. It's not the weather for... well, what you're wearing."

"Not freezing." She stared around as if she'd already lost interest in me. It's hard to imagine my style, grace, and charm could bore a person, but there's no accounting for taste. Regardless, I didn't see how she could deny how cold she must be; even with my alpaca t-shirt on, I was regretting offering her the hoodie, almost, and I hadn't been swimming in water that must have been even colder than the air.

"Well, let's put it on anyway, shall we?"

I shoved it towards her again, and she returned her attention to me, glanced down at the hoodie, then smiled. "Shall we?"

I took a deep breath while I tried to understand her answer, but she didn't reach for the hoodie. I rolled it up from the bottom, the way you do when you get yourself dressed, pushed my hands into the sleeves and held it closer to her. "Put it on, before you catch a cold." I gave her my warmest smile, although it didn't seem to warm her much, judging by her nipples.

I hadn't looked, and if I had, I don't admit it. They were hard to ignore, just poking out at me like two cigar butts, so okay, perhaps I did notice them. She still didn't take the hoodie, so I sighed my best frustrated mum sigh and tugged it over her head. She took a step backwards, but my daughter, Jo, had been the most wilful, belligerent kid ever, I swear, and one pathetic step backwards was no match for me. In that moment, the naked woman was a fat, lazy, domesticated cat who had gone into battle with the meanest, most vicious lioness in the jungle, and she was never going to win. We tussled, and at one point we both had an arm in one of the sleeves, but I'm not a quitter, and at last I had it over her body and tugged down as far as it would go without stretching. Hey, it was my hoodie, and I wanted it back in the same condition as when I lent it to her.

"There." The told-you-so I told-her-so with that one word. It had to be heard to be believed. They could probably see my triumphant smile from the top of Black Mountain. She looked a bit overwhelmed and stared at the hoodie as though it had appeared from nowhere. I caught the irony of that, since she, in fact, had appeared from nowhere.

She looked up and smiled, a lost, vulnerable smile with a hint of, "Sorry I broke your favourite vase/plate/vibrator, mum." I blushed; I admit it. I don't know why, but I felt that uncomfortable heat in my cheeks. I felt a bit guilty, even though I'd helped her. I'd forced my Mambo hoodie on her against her wishes. It wasn't her colour, it was baggy and ill-fitting, even on her catwalk figure, and there was a coffee stain just above the logo that was, if we're honest, her fault. I'm not a sloppy eater or drinker other than on the odd occasion I bump into a naked stranger.

"Why were you in the lake?" Why had I waited so long to try to learn what had happened to her? "Are you all right?" Damn. I'd already asked her that.

"All right." Damn. She'd already said that.

I took a deep breath. *"Stay calm, Abi. Don't scare her."* "Where do you live? Can I drop you home?"

She tilted her head to one side. The unblemished skin of

her forehead creased with the slightest frown, and she half-turned to point at the lake.

I wrinkled my far from unblemished forehead in a deep frown of confusion. Did she mean the lake? No, of course not. She had pointed to the University beyond it. She was a student; that made sense. A mature student who swam naked in the lake. "Can I drop you home, then?"

"What's going on here? Is she okay?" The man's voice made me jump, and my strange new friend covered her ears with her hands. I turned to look at him, a few years older than me, wrapped in a heavy coat, as though Anzac Day had come and gone weeks before.

Great. Just what I needed. Some nosey old bastard with no respect for Canberra traditions to mansplain how to look after the woman as he perved at her boobs. "She's fine. Just cold, that's all."

"She's soaking wet."

"*Well, aren't you Mr Observant?*" He had a grey-muzzled dog on a lead, some old multiple breed thing, the progeny of generations of horny ancestors rutting with whatever they came across in the streets of Belconnen in the days before dogs had to be microchipped, kept on a lead, and owners had to pick up their poop in a plastic bag. "She's fine, thanks."

"How did she get so wet?"

"*For fu...*" I blinked the long, slow blink of the terminally impatient as I battled my irritation. "She went for a swim." I glanced at her. She still had her hands pressed against her ears, sort of half stooped over, as though the debate distressed her. I reached out and rubbed her arm, high up near the shoulder; the safe zone. Abi Lucas, reassurance counsellor to the stars.

He rocked his head up, then back down, some sort of nod of

confirmation, as though he'd bought my answer hook, line, and sinker, to use an apposite fishing pun. "What's her name?"

What a stupid question. What did it matter to him what her bloody name was? "Kylie." I had to stifle a laugh. It was the first name I'd thought of, but it almost made me lol.

Kylie, or whatever, showed no sign of calming down, her hands pressed tight against her ears, and a dreadful thought ricocheted around my brain like a possessed pinball. The man seemed to worry her. Perhaps she'd been assaulted, or worse. I gripped her shoulders and said, "Come on, sweetheart. Let's take you somewhere safe where we can get you sorted out." My car was nearby, and I had a blanket in the boot. It had come from Kmart, but she was stuck with it. If she'd wanted something from some swanky store in the Canberra Centre, she should have picked a different rescuer.

"Safe." She stared at me, maybe in gratitude, maybe in doubt.

I pried one of the woman's hands away from the ear it had been attached to, then draped an arm around her shoulder. As I led her away, I called out to Mr Noseypants. "Thanks for the help." I didn't mean it. When we reached the path, I glanced back. The man had turned to watch, and so had his old dog. It barked once, a half-hearted, tragic sort of sound, as though it had apologised for its owner. "It's all good." The strange woman took her other hand away from her ear as I whispered my farewell to the mutt.

The car park at the boat ramp wasn't far, but the path around the lake had decided to send us half the population of Canberra now we were on the move, and everybody stared. Every. Single. Person. It was as if they'd never seen an almost fifty-year-old woman guide a younger one, saturated and dressed only in a jaded Mambo hoodie that barely reached below her hoo-ha, along the path before. We passed the kid's bicycle training park. Too early for any kids yet, thank the stars. Me and my barely dressed sidekick didn't have to worry about outraged parents. My lucky day.

It took about five anxious minutes to reach the car, a Mercedes A class hatch I'd bought two years ago with the insurance money, after... Never mind that. I fumbled the remote out of the bag draped across my body, unlocked the car, tugged the hatch open, and reached inside for the blanket.

The woman gasped and staggered backwards, and I grabbed for her in case she fell. She stared at me, wild-eyed, as though I had murdered the old man and eaten his dog raw, no barbecue sauce or anything. "It's okay, nothing to be afraid of. I'm just getting you a blanket to cover you up a bit and keep you warm." I tried to keep my voice soft and soothing, like years ago when Jo would wake in the night scared of a shadow on the wall. It's not so easy when you're dealing with a naked, mysterious woman who's just stepped out of a lake.

I turned back to the car, yanked the blanket out, and closed the hatch. When I draped the blanket around the woman, she was more cooperative, and I led her to the front passenger door. When I pulled it open, she gasped again and looked as though she was about to run away. "Why are you so scared of the car?"

The woman stopped and seemed relieved. "Car." She smiled. She had a beautiful smile, not that the poor thing had had much to smile about so far this morning.

Relieved she'd calmed down at last, I helped her into the car, went round it, got in myself, and heaved a long sigh. "Let's start again. My name's Abi. What's yours?"

The stranger smiled again. "Kylie."

2

I knew my mouth was open again, but I couldn't close it. I had become trapped in dropped-jaw hell. Either time stood still, or my facial muscles did. In the movies, the stranger would close my mouth with a finger under my chin, but all the woman did was grin and watch me flounder as I tried to unravel the knot my morning had wound itself into.

Her name might really be Kylie, but what are the chances of that? Only one other conclusion remained—she'd lied, repeated the name I'd used as a joke with the man. The silence wasn't awkward, but the next words I said could be, especially if I called her out on the lie I felt certain she'd told me. Everything about her was weird, from the fact she came out of the lake, naked, to the strange, truncated way she spoke, and now the name conundrum. It must be a prank. What other explanation could there be?

My phone rescued me, shattered the silence with a blast of

Christopher Cross's "Ride Like The Wind", the sample I'd put on my phone as my ringtone. Well, that's not true. Steve, Jo's husband, had done it for me, but I might have been able to do it myself. Who knows?

I pulled the phone out of my bag, still in my lap. The screen announced the caller. Jo. I had arranged to go shopping with her and Grace, my granddaughter. Instead, I'd bought my coffee and headed to the man-made beach beside the man-made lake for my occasional reflection session, and this woman had turned up. What a mess that had made of my morning. I pushed the green symbol to answer the call. "Hi, darling."

"Where are you? Are you all right?"

Everybody asking everybody else if they're all right. Not a good start to the day. "I'm in the car. There was"—what the hell could I say?—"an incident. A woman. In the lake—"

"In the lake? Had she drowned?"

"No, she's alive, but she needs help."

"Okay. What sort of help? CPR? Money? Help with her housework?"

Where did Jo get her sarcasm? Not from me, that's for sure. "Don't be silly. Just regular help." Outstanding repartee, Abi. Sharp as a football, that response.

"So, when will you be here?"

I glanced at Kylie, then closed my eyes and wished I hadn't just referred to her as Kylie in my mind. I sighed and blundered further down Idiot Lane. "I'll be late. I have to take her home, make sure she's okay."

Jo's silences could flay the skin from your bones from fifty paces, like razors or whirling blades, like the scene in *The Matrix*. Or had it been some other movie? I wasn't certain. I winced, ready for the retort. She wouldn't go easy on me just because I was her mother. "Home where? Why do you have to do it and not somebody else?"

That could have been so much worse. I'd dodged a bullet, really. I glanced up at the car roof and heaved a silent sigh of relief. "Because she's in my car, and I'm a good person." The "good person" card? I'd become desperate enough to fall back on that tired old line. It hadn't worked when I'd tried it before, and I doubted it would now.

Another silence. Unfair. Nobody should have to go through two of Jo's deathly silences in one phone call. That was the universe saying, "*You're the biggest loser. Goodbye.*" "Where are you? I'm coming down there. Are you still at the lake?"

I glanced at Kylie again. I couldn't let Jo loose on her. The poor woman looked as though her day had got off to a bad enough start already. Setting Jo on her would be the last straw. I might as well drag her back to the lake and drown her in the few minutes left to her. "We're just about to leave. I don't want to put you to any trouble, darling, and it's chilly this morning. Grace..." I ran out of steam like the balloon you find two days after the party, behind the lounge, wrinkled, deflated, looking like disappointment and unfulfilled dreams.

"Where are you taking her? The cops?"

The woman must have amazing hearing, because she cried out at that moment. "No cops."

Jo must have amazing hearing too. "Why doesn't she want the cops involved?"

My brain flailed around in search of something it could hang its hat on. If it wears a hat. I don't know for sure. "It's not that. I'm taking her home."

"Where to?"

"Tuggers. She's a Southsider." Too late, I realised I hadn't injected a Northsider's typical vitriol when referring to a denizen of the barren wasteland that lay beyond the bridge over Lake Burley Griffin.

A third silence? Had life saved up all my bad karma for this one moment? I felt tears well up, and I couldn't say whether they were tears of misery or fear at that moment. "Tuggers?"

"I have to go. She has an appointment at ten. I'll call you later. Love you." I disconnected.

It was a chicken move, I know that, but my heart had grabbed hold of my ribcage and shaken it so hard, I thought it would shatter. I couldn't endure a fourth silence. I'd never had to deal with three before. I wasn't equipped for a fourth. I would have run off screaming and persuaded the old dog to rip my throat out. I let out a long, unhappy sigh, turned to the woman, and gave her a confident smile. It didn't make either of us confident. "Where do you live?"

If she had said, "Tuggers," I might have torn my hoodie off her perfect body and kicked her out of the car. Instead, she gave another of those half-frowns, as though she feared a full frown might leave behind some spider-silk-thin hint of a wrinkle. "Lake."

I bit at the inside of my cheek. We were at a lake, and there were so many other lakes in Canberra. Why didn't she just say which one? *"Why is this so hard?"* I should just drive off, leave her here. Maybe it was only a dream. "Nobody lives in a lake, unless they're a fish. Where do you live?"

Nothing. She just looked at me with empty eyes while I struggled to understand any of it. What would Mike have done? Taken her to the cops, probably. He was more cynical and hard-nosed than me. That's where Jo got it from, I reckon.

The woman reached for me and wiped the tear from my cheek. I hadn't even realised it had dripped from my eye as Mike's face filled my thoughts, those deep brown eyes that said more than his mouth ever did, the smile that had never been far away, the laugh that always felt sympathetic even when you knew he really was laughing at you, not with you.

Why?

I sniffed and shook my head. This wouldn't do. It wasn't helping anyone. I couldn't take her to the cops naked, and I couldn't bear the thought of reclaiming my coffee-stained hoodie after they'd put her in an orange prison suit or whatever they did with her.

What had happened to my coffee? I didn't even remember what I'd done with it when she came out of the lake. A pang of guilt jolted through me at the thought I'd almost certainly left it on the ground somewhere. Litter bug. Old mate with the apologetic dog had probably already dobbed me in to the government. Some evil, malicious computer in the Department Of Scumbag Litterers would send me a letter with a photo of the evidence attached. I'd be fined, shamed by my lack of consideration for our fragile environment. I could never show my face again, I'd probably have to resign my membership of the Labor Club, and I'd have to resort to home delivery of food from the supermarkets instead of going to the store. Goodness only knew what Mrs Belt from number nine would make of the scandal. Maybe they'd make me do a walk of shame down Benjamin Way, like Cersei in Game Of Thrones.

I smiled at Kylie, embarrassed by the foolish train of thought I'd followed for a moment. "I'll take you to my house, hmm? We'll have a cup of tea, I'll find some clothes for you, then we'll work out what to do." That felt stupid. I didn't know her; why would I take her to my house? She might murder me, steal everything. Or not. Who knew?

Time to become that one person who would know. I started the car, turned the heat up for Kylie's benefit, and backed out of the space.

I don't think I've ever shaken with anxiety as much as I did on that short drive up the hill from the lake to our—my house. I'd lived in the house on Carson Street in Cook for over twenty-five years. Jo had been born soon after we moved in and had lived there until she married Steve four years ago and moved into the unit in Belconnen town centre. I'd told them they were too young, but they said they knew what they were doing, and it was what they wanted. Grace came along a year later, then a year after that...

The woman stared in awe at the giant owl who stands guard at the junction of Benjamin Way and Belconnen Way. "It's not real." I have no idea why I said that. It didn't look remotely real, and in fact was one of those love-it-or-hate-it representations of an owl. I like it; lots of people don't.

I shook myself out of the morbid thoughts again as I turned into the driveway and switched off the engine. Kylie hadn't looked very comfortable from the moment I started the car, and she sighed, visibly relaxed, and let go of the armrest on the door as the A Class's motor fell silent. I don't think I'm a bad driver, so her concern made no sense, just another piece of flammable material to throw on the bonfire of weirdness this morning had ignited in my life.

She'd had trouble putting the seatbelt on, and she had even more trouble taking it off. She tried to pull it over her head without unclicking the buckle, and I wondered whether she'd ever been in a car before. I had to go round to her side and help her in the end, or we'd have been there until Christmas, or she'd have hanged herself as she tried to get out of the car. That wouldn't look good on my rap sheet, if they even had those in Australia. More likely, I'd seen too many American cop series.

I took her indoors, sat her in an armchair, then fell onto the lounge, exhausted, terrified, anxious about her, worried I might have lost my mind. She gazed around, and her face reminded me of when I took Jo to the zoo for the first time. It seemed as though Kylie had never seen a television, a lounge, bookshelves, a coffee table, or a big wooden giraffe with flimsy legs, one broken and badly fixed, before. Mike. He loved that giraffe. I hated it, but I couldn't throw it out now. For the record, the giraffes at the zoo are real and have functioning legs.

She reached for the book on the coffee table, "*A World Of Ashe And Ember*." I'd bought it from a lovely woman at the Haig Park market in Braddon a couple of weeks before. Kylie stared at the cover, entranced. She read the title aloud, and she turned to me, her head on one side, the little frown on her forehead.

"It's fantasy." What else could I say? The author had published it herself, she'd said. I'd only started it a few nights ago and hadn't got far yet, so I couldn't tell her much about it. I had thought the title was a typo, but it turned out Ashe and Ember were the two women in the story. They were a couple, and they had sex a lot, as I found out early in the book. I hadn't realised that when I bought it, but love is love, and I'm the last person to discriminate against anyone for being in love.

Kylie—why couldn't I stop calling her that? The woman took the book in her hand, opened it at the first page, then sort of flicked through the pages, the book wide open in her hands. Her eyes moved non-stop as she fanned from one page to the next. It took maybe eight seconds. She looked up at me. "It's good. I like it a lot. I like how the title is about the two women and not a mistake. Do you like it?"

I knew my mouth was open again, but I'd given up on it by now. She must have already read the book. Perhaps she'd been at the market too. Nobody reads a book in eight seconds. And all those words she'd said. She hadn't used that many words all morning until she spoke about the book. She must have already read it. "Have you already read it?"

"Yes. You saw me read it. Do you have any more?" She looked around, then stood and went to the bookshelves. I turned to watch as she ran her hands along the spines of the books on one shelf. "This is what I need." She reached up, and my sweatshirt rode up over her bum, which treated me to a plumber's smile, even though she probably wasn't a plumber.

I only felt the dribble when it dripped from my chin onto the back of my hand. I closed my mouth and wiped the rest of the drool from my chin with the back of the hand. Embarrassing, but she hadn't noticed, thank goodness. Her smile stretched the width of the room as she waved the dictionary in front of her in triumph, like a gladiator in the Coliseum waving the head of his vanquished foe, but without the ick factor. She repeated the page flick, and this one took a lot longer. Close to fifteen seconds, I reckon, and she had to go back and re-flick in a couple of places. As she flicked, I realised she'd pulled out the Stage Two Frown. Much deeper than the ones I'd seen so far, but still not what I would call a WTAF frown. I got that frown from Jo, a lot.

She put the dictionary back and turned towards me with a huge grin on her face. "Excellent. You mentioned a cup of tea, I think. I'd love to try one, please."

I stared at her. She stared at me. Who was this woman? She could barely say, "Boo," to a goose half an hour ago, but now she was like a dripping tap, chatting away nineteen to the dozen and flicking through books. What on earth had happened?

"Are you all right, Abi?"

The question snapped me back to some kind of reality, but now the world really had turned upside down. She had asked me if I was all right, when earlier in the day she'd been the one who seemed all broken and bewildered. I shook my head. It always works in the movies, but nothing made any more sense after the shake, and some more dribble flew off my chin to land on the carpet. Disappointing. "Cup of tea. Right. Milk and sugar?"

Just the Stage One Frown this time. "No thank you. I don't consume animals."

A vegetarian. Who am I to judge? I admire their principles and their commitment. I can't stand to think of the animals suffering, and on the freeway, I hate passing those horrible trucks packed with the poor things, but I still eat them. I'd just make her a cup of black tea, as soon as I thought my legs could be trusted to hold me up, and my body stopped shaking like a jelly in an earthquake.

She pulled another book from the bookshelf, flicked through it, then held it towards me with a look that implied she hadn't enjoyed it as much as the dictionary. Why would she, after all? Even I hadn't read the book about the history of the Holden Commodore. Jo had got it for one of Mike's birthdays. "Not much of a story?" Why had I asked her that? There was no story, unless you were obsessed with old cars, like Mike had been.

"It's non-fiction." She was on to me, knew I'd asked a pathetic question and decided to belittle me even more than I'd already done. "It's the history of the iconic Commodore and the role it's played in the fabric of Australian motoring—"

I held up a hand. She'd gone too far. I wanted to come out of this with some small scrap of dignity intact somewhere within me. The time had come for me to take control, assert some dominance, prove this was my home, and nobody trifled with me in my own home. "I'll make us that tea, then."

4

"This is nice." Kylie had heeded my advice and allowed the tea to cool for a while before she drank it, but then she had skulled it like a racing car driver doing a shoey. I'd taken two sips of mine, even though the milk would have made mine cooler. I didn't mention the milk. I didn't want an argument.

"Where do you live? I'll take you home." I know I'd asked before, but maybe she'd learned where she lived now she'd read the dictionary. I'd gone down the rabbit hole this morning, and if you're going down that hole, do it with style, that's my mantra.

"The lake, the one that was empty."

I frowned. Stage Four, at least. "Lake George?"

"Yes, there. I live there. Can you take me?"

How could I make some sense of all this? I needed to, or I'd go bonkers. Whatever lay behind all this weirdness, I felt she owed me some kind of explanation before I drove her all the way out to Lake George. There weren't many houses out that way, but that was none of my business. "Why were you in the lake this morning? Where are your clothes?"

Kylie twisted her mouth up in one corner, as though she thought hard about how to answer a difficult question, such as, "Where are your clothes?" She smiled before she answered. "My clothes are at home. I took a swim in the lake, and now I need to go home."

Throughout the long ages of time, of all the answers that weren't answers, that was the most non-answer that ever wasn't an answer. I decided to call her out. "How did you get into the lake? How did you get to Belco from Lake George?"

"Car."

"What car?"

"Commodore. VF Two. Best ever."

Mike had always said the VT was the best, but I let her ignorance slide. "Where is it now, then, this Commodore?"

She hesitated. I had her, like a rat in a trap. That analogy grossed me out a bit, and I wished I hadn't thought it. Or was it a simile? What is wrong with me? "Home."

I gave her my most disarming smile, but her arms didn't fall off. "I think you'll find the VF Two didn't have any self-driving capability. An expert would know that." Anybody would know it, let's face it. That stuff had barely been rolled out yet, and it wasn't legal to use anyway.

"Brother."

Damn, she'd out-manoeuvred me. I'd fallen into her trap just when I thought I had her in mine. Down, but not out, I countered. "Fine. Let's call him. Perhaps he can drive the Commodore back in to pick you up."

"He's at work."

The car thing had completed its final lap, I thought, so I

returned to the clothes. "Did he take your clothes back with him?"

She nodded. "He did. As a prank."

Had I just fed her that line? It felt that way, but it also felt like I was arguing with an encyclopaedia, and I didn't have the patience for it. "Fine. I'll find you some clothes and take you home." I stood.

"You're very kind, Abi. Thank you for helping me."

That threw me. I had not anticipated that line at all, and I sank back onto the lounge. I knew my cheeks were red because they were piping hot. "It's all right. Think nothing of it." Another thought occurred to me. I sensed I would regret it, but it shot out, one of those, "I was just thinking that, then I said it," moments. "What's your real name?"

"Kylie. How did you know that, by the way?"

Cunning, and I admired it. She'd avoided the question and turned it back on me. "Just a lucky guess." I had only been thinking that one, but I'd still said it.

"You must be very lucky, then."

"*Not so much these days, my dear. Once upon a time, yes, but now...*" I sniffed back another tear.

She held out a hand towards me. "Are you all right? Did I upset you?"

"No, it's not your fault. I'm sorry. I just thought about Mike."

"Mike?"

"My husband. He died a couple of years ago." The tears came faster, thicker, and I buried my face in my hands, alarmed by the speed at which I'd deteriorated into this blubbering mess.

"I'm sorry to hear that. You seem young for a widow. The average age for a widow is sixty-nine."

I sort of cry-laughed, miserable, but amused. She did speak like an encyclopaedia. "Where did you hear that?"

"In your encyclopaedia."

I looked up and frowned. I think I gave her the WTAF frown, if I'm honest. "In my encyclopaedia? That thing there?" I pointed at it, and she nodded. "It's ancient. It might be thirty years old." Another thought occurred to me. "When did you read my encyclopaedia?"

"While you were making the tea. I read all your books."

"You read all my..." I shook my head, baffled. "I'm forty-nine." She didn't reply, but she looked confused. "How old are you?"

She huffed out a breath, as though the question had caught her out. How old are you? What's the square root of pi multiplied by the sum of the square of the other two sides and divided by the average age of a widow, minus my age? Equally difficult questions, so I gave her a moment's grace. "Thirty-one."

She didn't look thirty-one now she had dried, but then I really looked at her. She could be twenty or a hundred and twenty. She had perfect skin, beautiful, long, glowing hair, a figure I would have killed for at any time in my life, slender, fine hands with long fingers. Behind her eyes, despite the perfect physical package, the worries of the ages could be detected if you looked for long enough.

Long enough to embarrass your guest, as it turned out. "What?"

I looked away, ashamed. "Nothing. I'm sorry, I didn't mean to stare."

"It's fine. Tell me about your husband."

I hadn't expected that and didn't know what to say. A complete stranger comes into your life and asks about something like that, it throws you for a loop. Two hours ago, I didn't know her from any of the other fish in Lake Ginninderra, but here she was, asking me about Mike.

I didn't quite know how much to reveal, so I took the safe route and told her every single thing. How we'd met when I was a freshly minted accountant working at a small firm in the city. Mike worked for one of the global giants, and they wanted to buy the little firm I worked for. He came down from Sydney as part of their acquisitions and mergers team. We hit it off right away, got on like the proverbial house on fire, and we started seeing each other. When he had to go back to Sydney, the deal done, we didn't know what to do, so we carried on a long-distance relationship for a few months. I'd go there for the weekend, or he'd come here.

He asked me to marry him. I wanted to, but I hated Sydney, so he pulled some strings and got a transfer to the Canberra office. We got married, bought the house, had Jo, then decided to leave the firm and set up by ourselves. We were good; lots of regular clients, grew to a good size, then the same global giant came calling. They offered us so much money, we'd have been mad to turn it down. We retired.

Grace was born, and it was perfect. We had all the time in the world to spend with our first granddaughter. Time. You've got plenty of it on your hands until you haven't. Or rather, in this case, until some drunk driver decides you haven't. Mike was gone, just like that. The cops came to the door, and my life shattered into a million pieces.

I stopped, tired of the tears, tired of the what-ifs, the whys.

Two years had gone by, but I still missed him. I hadn't even got rid of his clothes. I hadn't forgiven the bastard who smashed into him, and I doubted I ever would. Can't be a good person all the time, right?

Kylie wiped at her eyes. "That's a sad story."

"*Bit of an understatement there, girl.*" I nodded, hopeless, because I didn't know what else to say. Jo had taken it hard. She'd always been rough around the edges, but she got worse after Mike was killed. I did what I could to help, but when you're in pieces yourself, it's pretty difficult to stick someone else back together. "Thank you." I couldn't think of anything else to say. The mood had turned as black as the deepest night, and I needed some air. "Do you fancy a walk?"

She hesitated, and I guessed she wanted to go home, then she smiled. "Where to?"

"Just up to the top of the hill and back. Lovely views from up there." It's only a hill, Mount Painter, but it's an invigorating climb up there, and so worth it as you gaze around you. It's sometimes hard to look out over Black Mountain, Lake Burley Griffin, and the Arboretum and remember you're in the nation's capital. It's beautiful, and I needed it right then.

"Let's go."

She stood. Barefooted. Left her hiking boots in the back of the brother's Commodore, I imagined, then felt guilty. I loaned her an old pair of sneakers. They were a bit big, but a pair of Mike's thick footie socks did the trick. Her feet were dainty, like her hands, and not at all like my ugly troll's feet. A pair of my old track pants and a t-shirt, one of my old jackets that was far too big for her, and she looked the part, ready to tackle the hill.

It's a fair climb up Mount Painter, even though my house is already part of the way up. By the time we got to the top, I was puffing a bit. I'd been a lot fitter before Mike was killed. Kylie, of course, hadn't been tested by it at all. Her heart rate had probably gone down, if anything. She turned slow circles, her eyes closed, her arms out from her sides, her hair blowing in the stiff breeze that had sprung up. She looked like Jo the first time we brought her up here, when she'd been about five. Enthralled, captivated by the scenery, as though she'd never seen anything like it before. Strange, for someone who claimed to live out at Lake George, where it's pretty bushy, and pretty lakey.

We sat for a while on the big rock near the trig station. Like me, she was disappointed at the new development at Molonglo. More of the natural land eroded by huge housing estates, reaching further and further out to spill the city westwards in an endless quest for more rates that never seemed enough to support the required infrastructure and needed more development, as Catch-22 as it gets. As we chatted about it, I suspected she might be one of those eco-warriors, a Greta Thunberg type, almost. I had no issue with that. I wasn't the greatest at being green, but I wasn't the worst. I'd signed up for the FOGO trial and threw all my food waste into the green bin. I should have done more with the garden, but that had always been Mike's passion, not mine.

I couldn't prise any more useful information about her life out of her, and when I looked at my watch, it was almost four o'clock. I don't know why, but despite the strangeness, the weird way she had appeared, the bizarre claims about reading books by flicking through them, the fact-based way she spoke, I felt comfortable with her. I'd had a hard time with my friends after the accident. They'd tried to console me, be there for me, but most of them had smothered me, and I hadn't enjoyed it.

This weirdo knew nothing about me, and it felt good. It felt fresh, like we could talk about something without Mike's shadow over us, without having to choose our words so we didn't start each other crying about the tragedy that night. That terrible night.

"Let's head back. I'll cook us something for dinner. I can take you home after, if you like, or you can stay the night." Oh my god, why had I added that? What an idiot.

She raised her chin, a sort of acknowledgement of what I'd said. "How far is it?"

"To Lake George?" She nodded. "You don't know how far it is?"

She looked down, stared at the ground for a time while I tried to unravel the peculiar question. When she looked up again, I thought I saw doubt in her eyes. "I don't drive. I've never noticed."

What a load of crap. Although she had no watch on... *"Come on Abi. Don't be stupid."* I poised for an attack, like a snake, ready to lunge, to bury my fangs in her flesh and inject the venom of sarcasm. I couldn't do it. Don't ask me why, but I couldn't put her to the sword in that minute. "Half an hour or so, the way I drive. Bit more, probably."

I gave her my most reassuring smile, but she didn't seem very reassured. She drew in a long breath. "Maybe we can go tomorrow. I'd like to talk to you some more. You're nice."

"*Nice?*" Nice is a terrible compliment. It's like saying, "There's nobody else around for five hundred kilometres, so you'll do." "Thank you. Let's head down." I stood, then paused. "You don't eat meat?"

"I don't. I can't eat animals."

I let the "can't" go. Too nuanced, and I'd run out of today's energy for any more attempts to pry this woman open and spill her secrets around me. I'd find a vegetarian recipe in one of my books and make that. I had no idea what they ate. I don't think I'd ever had a vegetarian friend, come to think of it. "We'll figure it out one way or the other."

She smiled, and her perfect skin seemed even more radiant. Probably a bit of windburn.

5

We decided on aloo gobi. When I say "we," I mean "I," because it looked easy to cook and I'd enjoyed it before at Indian restaurants. Kylie had no opinion either way and claimed never to have had a curry in her life. I found it difficult to believe somebody who'd lived for thirty-one years had never eaten a curry, but when I went to say so, I remembered the rest of the day. Honestly, that seemed fairly normal compared to everything else that had happened since this morning, so I settled for an understanding smile, which didn't help me understand any of it.

I had potatoes, I had cauliflower, I had tomatoes, I had rice, and I had some spices. It took maybe half an hour to prepare, and I served it up just like the art-on-a-plate you get in those high-end restaurants. Okay, I spooned it out over the rice, and some of it fell on the floor. I cracked the same joke Mike and I always used whenever one of us dropped or spilled some food or drink. "Oops, I've dropped some of yours."

"It's okay. I'm sure there's plenty."

Another thing learned. She had no sense of humour. "Do you need a comb?"

She stared at me, a blank expression, as though I was the strange one in the kitchen, not her. "I don't understand. Why would I need a comb?"

"So you can comb your hair. I think it got messed up by my joke as it flew over your head."

She reached up to the top of her perfect blonde hair. "Really?"

If I had quit after the "some of yours" comment, I would only be down one of my favourite jokes instead of two. Both had landed on woefully barren ground, my unquestionable humour wasted on a Philistine with no ear for a joke.

I forced cheeriness into my voice, although it sounded more like a high-pitched squeak of resignation. "Never mind. Let's eat."

I wiped up the mess. I'm a tidy person trapped in the body of a forty-nine-year-old, "I'll pick it up later," woman, but I needed to impress Kylie and didn't want the next person who called round to find the aloo gobi congealed on the kitchen floor, so I did the right thing. Brava Abi.

From her first mouthful, I had five Michelin stars. I had a glittering new career ahead of me as one of those genius but unpleasant television chefs. If there was a World Cup of cooking, I'd just won it. To say Kylie loved it would not do her reaction justice. She picked up a scoop of the meal on her fork, blew on it, as you do, popped it between her red, plump, perfect lips, and sighed—no, cooed—in ecstasy. Her clear, green eyes widened so far I think they might have created a permanent wrinkle in that hitherto unblemished forehead. "OMG. That is so good."

I blushed. From the praise, for the most part, but also from the cringe. Who says, "OMG?" Everybody texts it, of course, but nobody says it, not in the circles I move in, at least. "OMG? Where did you learn that?"

"From one of your books."

"Do you learn everything from books? Didn't your parents teach you anything?" She looked down and seemed embarrassed. I felt guilty for my rudeness and remembered I'd told Jo I was a good person earlier in the day. That hadn't lasted long. "I'm sorry, that was rude of me. Which book?"

"I forget." She gave a girlish giggle, as though I'd caught her sneaking a bit of my curry onto her plate. "I read so many."

I put my fork down and stared at her through the steam that rose from our plates. Earlier, I'd run out of energy for the mystery this woman represented, but it had found its second wind. "Okay, let's talk about that. What is this thing you do? You flick through a book, then claim you've read it. Why do you do that?"

She looked put out, and my guiltometer cranked up a notch. "I do read them. That's how to read. Isn't that how you read?"

I snort-laughed. "No. Nobody does."

"Oh." She stared down at her lap again as she fiddled with a strand of hair. I didn't know what to do or say, but she looked up at me. "I do."

I told myself to get a grip. Nothing unusual here; she's just a speed reader. Except that's not speed reading, that's freakish, if it could even be done. "How is that possible?"

"How is it not?"

Good question. I imagined it would be impossible to absorb so many words in such a short time even if she did somehow see them all, but how could I prove it beyond a doubt? I couldn't, and that was her responsibility in any case. "Prove it."

I might have sounded a bit confrontational, but she sat upright and looked happier. "How?"

"Have you been in my bedroom?"

She looked horrified. "No."

I jumped up and ran to my room. I dug around in my wardrobe and pulled an old copy of *Frankenstein* out of the box of Mike's old books. I hadn't thrown any of them away, either, like the clothes. I couldn't store them all on the shelves, and I'd left the ones I didn't think I'd read in the box. I hurried back to the table and handed it to her. "Read this."

She flicked through it, and I held out my hand. When she passed the book over, I cracked it open. "What's the first line on page 63?"

"It's part of a sentence in a letter from Frankenstein's adopted cousin. 'his elder brother returns to us.'"

How did she know that? "Have you read this before?" She shook her head. "First line of chapter twenty?"

"'I sat one evening in my laboratory; the sun had—'"

"Okay, enough. Are you sure you haven't read this?" She gave me an enthusiastic nod. I sighed. "You flicked through it, read it in a heartbeat, but can recall every word?"

"Yes. Is that odd? It's very good, by the way."

"Of course it's good. It's a classic."

"The language is complex, far more than the modern books I've read. It's interesting how language has changed so much in two hundred years."

I blew a raspberry sound from my lips. "If you say so. I've never read it. It was Mike's book, really."

"She published the first edition anonymously because—"

I stifled a yawn. I'm so polite. "I know, I know. I suppose you read that in the encyclopaedia."

"I did." The enthusiasm had drained from her voice and her face. She could read a book in a few seconds and, it seemed, had a photographic memory for every word she read. Even an encyclopaedia. I didn't know how to react to that revelation, so I took a mouthful of food. Kylie followed my example, and we ate in silence for a time. She put her fork down and gave me an earnest look. "This food is better than *Frankenstein*."

A tear dripped into the remnants of my aloo gobi.

6

"I need a glass of wine. This has been a day." I wiped at my eyes, stood, and picked up my plate. Kylie hadn't finished, so I headed into the kitchen, pulled a bottle of pinot noir out of the wine fridge, and took two glasses out of the cupboard. I poured wine into each glass, then stood and stared at the light red liquid. I hadn't asked her about wine; she might not drink or might only drink wine that conformed to some ecologically sound terroir.

"What are you doing, Abi? Why have you invited this woman into your home despite all those red flags waving in front of you all day?" I didn't know, the simple truth. Kylie seemed in need of help, but I couldn't work out what sort of help she needed. She went from two-word answers to a walking fount of knowledge with a ten second flick through a book. She'd never had a curry, wouldn't tell me her name or where she lived. I should have taken her straight to the cops. I'd driven past the station on the way home from the lake and hadn't even made

Mike's favourite old comment in my mind. "*You'll never take me alive, copper.*" Instead, here I stood, about to offer her a glass of wine after I'd cooked her a dinner, a total stranger who was to normal what The Seekers were to heavy metal.

"What's wrong?" Her voice made me jump. I turned as she put her plate on the counter, concern in her eyes. I couldn't remember seeing much emotion on her face all day, but as she looked at me, I felt the need to unburden myself of so much, and who better than a stranger who seemed not to have known a bloody thing until she read my encyclopaedia?

"Nothing, sorry. Just lost in my thoughts. Can you put that in the dishwasher please?"

As her eyes swept the kitchen, another realisation dawned. Nothing could surprise me any more, so I reached past her and pulled the dishwasher door open. She gave me a sheepish grin and laid the plate on the bottom rack. I muttered something about having to teach her everything and stood the plate up next to my own.

I carried the glasses out of the kitchen, put them on the coffee table, and flopped down on the lounge. "Take a seat. I poured you a glass too. I need it, but if you don't drink, that's fine."

"I've never had wine."

I waved a hand in the air. Of course she hadn't. Why would she? There were a couple of vineyards out at Lake George, and I'd assumed she lived on one of them, but she'd never had a glass of wine in her life. "If you don't like it, I'll finish it."

Kylie sat in the chair opposite me and picked up one of the glasses. She tested the wine's nose. To be fair, it was more a case of sniffing it with blatant suspicion, and she made no insightful observations such as, "Notes of sweaty saddle." Tentative, like a prisoner invited to sit and who's been told it's just a massage chair, she raised the glass to her lips, hesitated, glanced over at me, lowered her head, sniffed again, then, mere seconds before I screamed at her to drink the bloody stuff, she took a speculative sip.

She placed the glass back on the table, a gentle, smooth action that barely disturbed the surface of the cheerful red liquid in it. I waited. I waited some more. I stopped waiting. "Well?"

"It's very nice. I like it."

"What would the encyclopaedia say about it?"

She stared at the ceiling for a moment, then returned her gaze to me. "It would say things about the palate and the finish, the fruits and the notes."

"Nothing more specific than that?"

"Nothing I can think of."

I sat up and took a sip. "I can taste cherry, maybe strawberry too."

"I see."

"Didn't you taste them too?"

"I've never had any of those things, so I couldn't say. It's lovely though. Thank you for pouring me some." She lifted the glass and took a longer pull of the pinot.

Yay me. My jaw hadn't dropped. Who has never had a strawberry? I took a deep drink of the wine. "You've led a strange life."

She muttered into her glass. "You have no idea."

"No, Kylie, I don't have any idea, because you haven't really told me a damn thing about yourself."

She took another drink. "I'm sorry. I can't tell you anything. There isn't much to tell, and you wouldn't believe it anyway."

"That's a bit creepy, and a bit condescending." Another drink. My glass was half empty already.

I couldn't see any deception or threat in her face, just earnestness and that same sense of lostness. "I'm not creepy. I'm no threat. Quite the opposite."

I didn't know what to make of that, so I went to the kitchen for the bottle and topped us up. "Why should I believe that?" Why had I invited her into my home if I didn't know whether to believe she posed any threat? The truth was, I hadn't felt any menace from her. She frustrated me, sure, but in a weird way, I liked her. I saw some of my own confusion and stumbles in her, I think.

Glass in hand, she leaned back in the chair. "Tell me more about Mike."

"What else is there to tell? We got married when I was twenty-three and were married for twenty-four years before he was killed. We had Jo when I was twenty-five. Hard work and good fortune meant we could retire young. I was only forty-six, Mike was fifty. It was a dream, then it was a nightmare."

"You must have been very happy until that day."

"Most of the time." I took another long drink. "He wasn't without his faults."

"Are you?"

I laughed. "Shut up. No, of course not. Nobody is, but at least I never..." *Don't go there, Abi. Don't tell her about that.*

"What does that mean?"

She was keeping pace with me, matching me drink for drink. The ideal opportunity to deflect the conversation away from the uncomfortable direction it had headed in. "Slow down, girlie. If you've never drunk before, you might want to go easy. You'll be pissed before you know it."

"Pissed?"

"Drunk. Wine makes you drunk. It helps you forget things."

"That sounds good."

I sighed, raised the glass to my lips, then paused. "It can be, but you only forget for a little while. The next day, nothing's changed, and you feel like shit."

"If you're going to feel like shit, so am I." She swallowed more of the garnet liquid, and I gave up and took another mouthful.

"On your head be it. I'm used to it, but you'll be sorry in the morning."

"What do you mean, you're used to it?"

I hesitated. Why did I feel compelled to be so honest with this woman? What if she was a reporter from the Canberra Times, come to expose all my hideous secrets? I laughed at that. My hideous secrets weren't worth the effort. Lazier than I should be with housework, drank more wine than I should, had a complicated relationship with my daughter. No real skeletons in my closet. Unlike Mike. "I drink more wine than I should these days. At nights, alone here, nobody to talk to, it helps. Keeps some of the memories away."

She nodded, like some sage old wise woman, but she couldn't know a thing about how the nights were for me. "You have someone to talk to tonight."

I tipped the last of the wine into our glasses and nodded at Kylie's. "Don't say I didn't warn you."

Her laughter danced around the room. Laughter had been in scarce supply in this house in recent times, and it sounded good to hear some. "I understand. It's my own fault. What memories do you want to keep away?"

I studied her over the rim of my glass. A rosy hue had come to her cheeks; the wine, I guessed. "I'll tell you what, why don't you tell me something for a change? What's your real name?"

"Kylie."

The joke had worn thin by now. I wouldn't have said I'd grown tired of it, but I would have valued some honesty. "Kylie what?" Maybe that would get some more information out of her.

"Yes."

"What do you mean, 'yes?'"

"My name. It's Kylie Watt."

Preposterous. "What game are you playing, Kylie? What do you want from me?"

"I don't want anything from you, although you've already given me so much. You're special, not like I expected." She fell silent and glanced down at her lap, as though she had let something slip, something unintended.

I chewed at my bottom lip. Everything she said seemed strange, obscure, as if she used the clues from a difficult crossword puzzle as her basis of speech. "What did you expect?"

"Are all the up... Are all the humans like you?"

I leaned forward, all attention and aroused curiosity, not that the entire day hadn't been one long curiosity. "All the what? Up?"

"I misspoke. The wine."

In the back of my mind, something about the way she had worded the question rang an alarm bell I couldn't quite find the reason for. The slip about up-something was one thing, but something else bubbled underneath that. It came to me. "All *the* humans? Why would you ask what *the* humans are like? Are you some kind of spaceman? Woman?"

She laughed, and I must confess, I felt a bit stupid for asking such a strange question. "I must be drunk. You said I would be. I meant the people in this area. Are they all like you?"

"And how am I, exactly?"

She didn't hesitate. "Kind, friendly, helpful. A good person, like you told the person on the... Earlier."

You wouldn't read about it, would you? Kylie didn't know what a phone was. What a surprise. I snorted. "No."

"No? What do you mean?"

"People aren't the things you said. I'm not those things either. You're drunk."

"Thank you, anyway. You helped me, whether you're a good person or not."

I couldn't stand much more of this praise. The stupid woman knew nothing about me, but she thought I was Mother Teresa. I went to the kitchen and brought out another bottle of wine. "I'm not sure you should have any more. You're as drunk as a skunk."

She giggled on cue. "Do you still want me to stay, or will you take me home?"

"I can't drive you after half a bottle of wine, so you'll have to stay." I added another glass to the reason not to drive, then hovered the bottle over her glass, gave her a questioning look.

"I'll take some more. Please."

I filled her glass.

7

The phone woke me up. I felt every bit as shit as I'd promised Kylie she would feel, but unlike her, this wasn't my first rodeo. I scrabbled around for my phone. Jo. Bugger. I pushed the green symbol. "Hi kiddo."

"Hi mum. I wondered if you'd like to come shopping today, since you missed out yesterday."

"Oh, right. Sorry about that." I pressed a hand to my forehead as though I could relieve my headache through some osmosis. Would it be osmosis? I'd forgotten my chemistry lessons from school, and dwarves were mining precious metals in my frontal lobe, so I had no hope of resolving the conundrum.

"What did the cops say when you took her in, by the way?"

"Nothing. I didn't take her to the cops."

A silence this early, and with a hangover? Come on. "What did you do with her?"

"What did I do with her? I didn't do anything with her. I brought her home, loaned her some clothes, and gave her a meal." And a gutful of pinot noir, but Jo needn't know anything about that. I'd already had my silence for the day.

"Then...?"

"She stayed the night. She's in your bed."

"She's still in bed? It's almost ten o'clock."

"*Get the front door.*" I pulled the phone away from my ear. She was right. Damn. How had I slept so late?

"She's in your room, I meant. Hasn't come out yet." Neither had I, but Jo didn't need to know that. What the head doesn't know, the heart can't grieve over.

"So, are you taking her to the cops today?"

"Yes. No. I don't know. She lives out at Lake George. I might drop her out there."

"I thought she lived in Tuggers?"

I'd said that, hadn't I? Damn. "No, that was a misunderstanding. Lake George."

"What's her name?"

Oh shit. Why ask me that? I didn't want to answer. "You know what? I'll get her up, give her some brekkie, then I'll drive her out to the lake. I'll call you when I'm back, okay? Bye, love. Kiss Gracie for me."

I hung up before Jo could get started. I was in no shape for her attitude. I got out of bed. By that, I mean I oozed from between the sheets like a kid squeezing toothpaste onto a toothbrush and missing. I collapsed to my knees, cursed Dionysus, Bacchus, and every other bloody god of wine throughout all mythology, took a deep breath, and pushed myself upwards until I swayed, but I was upright.

Walls and doors. Thank the stars for them, or I would have fallen half a dozen times between my bedroom and the kitchen, including the return for my dressing gown when I realised I was naked. I'd turned back before the lounge, lucky for me, because I'd maligned Kylie. She was sitting in the same chair she'd been in last night. She looked up as I slithered into view, a sack of impending projectile vomit constrained by more flesh than there used to be.

"Morning." I muttered the greeting under my breath as I slid my upper body along the counter towards the tap of life-giving water.

"Good morning. How do you feel? I am quite hungover, I think, as you promised me I would be."

Anybody who could muster that many cheerful words wasn't hungover. Was she some demon come to haunt my last days? Based on how I felt, she would be out of work by this evening. "Good for you. I feel terrible." I ran some water into a glass, took a sip, and felt it gurgle around in my stomach, where I presumed it fell, valiant, into the vast amount of wine, like the three hundred Spartans under the million Persian arrows. Unlike the battle of Thermopylae, my Persians didn't hurl the Spartans back where they came from, but I leaned over the sink, unsure the water hadn't started a reaction that would rival Pompeii in its power, its tragic consequences, and the extent of its coverage.

"Will you show me how to make tea? I'll make us both a cup. You seem as though you could use it."

I didn't raise my head from the sink. My voice had a metallic, echoey quality as a result. "You don't know how to make tea?"

Kylie hesitated. "I've forgotten."

I would have laughed, if I hadn't been so afraid my laughter would be liquid and filled with peas and carrots I hadn't eaten. I heaved out a long breath instead. That would have to suffice for now. "I'll show you in a minute."

"Are you ill? Shall I try to find help?"

I waved a feeble hand at her and struggled to the lounge. Jabba The Hut would have settled on that lounge with more dignity than I did, but I was horizontal again. My stomach rejoiced by gurgling in a threatening manner, but it stayed put. For now.

Kylie hovered over me, like Mike used to whenever I was crook. Unlike then, I had no obligations today. I didn't have a toddler to raise or tax returns to file, audits to attend. Back then, I had to shake it off, get back on the paddock and play my best game every day, sick or not. Today, I was in no shape to do much of anything, including drive to Lake George. She had concern in her voice. "You look ill. Would you like to walk up to Mount Painter again for some fresh air? It might help."

"Are you serious? I made it to the lounge. What more do you want from me?" I squinted up at her. "No thanks, sweetheart. You go though, if you want to. Do you think you can find the way?"

Frown, Stage One. "I think so."

"Good. If you get lost, ask someone to take you to the cops. They'll ring your home or—"

"No cops."

The urgency in her voice, the fear, made me open my eyes fully and take notice. She'd said the same yesterday. I'd dismissed it then, but now it made no sense. Unless she was a criminal. What if she was a mass murderer who lured her victims into a pretend friendship, then dismembered them and buried them in their own back yard? To be honest, that didn't seem so bad compared to how I felt at that moment. "Why no cops?"

"I just... I can't explain it. I'm afraid of them."

There was always a hint of some story I couldn't be sure I wanted to hear behind everything she said. Had a cop mistreated her? Had somebody attacked her, hurt her, and the cops treated her like it had all been her fault? Rumours said they did that, so maybe. "Why are you afraid of them?"

"Abi, I like you, I do. I'm not being disrespectful or ungrateful, but I can't tell you. Please don't ask."

I didn't need an argument, but I did need more sleep. "Fine. No cops. If you're lost, ask someone to tell you where thirty Carson Street is. That's here. Have fun."

"What about the tea?"

"I'll show you when you're back."

Kylie stood there for some time, then turned away. I shut my eyes, heard the door close as she left the house, and fell asleep.

I woke an hour or so later. Kylie wasn't back, and part of me hoped she wouldn't come back. I'd be down some clothes, but I'd be free of the strangeness, free to go back to my life. My lonely, pointless existence, the wine, the regrets, the memories, the cantankerous daughter who blamed me for her father's death because I'd had a couple of glasses of wine that night, so Mike drove them all home. He dropped them off, but he never made it back.

I struggled into my room and took a shower. A shower only washes your outside, unless you swallow all the water, I suppose, but it makes you feel good inside too. Okay, "good" was a stretch, but I felt better, at least.

I dressed and went out to the kitchen. I felt hungry, so I made a piece of toast, buttered it, and sat on the lounge with it and a cup of tea. Kylie hadn't returned, almost two hours later, and I felt guilty. What if she had fallen and hurt herself? What if she hadn't known what a kangaroo was, asked one for directions to thirty Carson Street, and got into a boxing match with it?

The door opened, and I exhaled a sigh of relief. I heard a few whispered words and wondered why she had spoken so quietly. "Kylie?"

"Hello Abi." She hadn't come into the lounge, so I stood. What was she up to? I took a step towards the hallway, and she walked into the room.

She wasn't alone. She was, however, the only one of the pair wearing clothes. Another naked woman? Two days running? Were the ACT Government breeding them, some horrific experiment to create an army of beautiful, flawless, naked warriors? This one had brown hair, not quite as tall as Kylie, but as perfect as her, two Barbie dolls side by side. I took a hesitant step backwards and collapsed onto the lounge. "Who's this?"

Kylie shuffled her feet. I never trust people who shuffle their feet. Villains in books and movies always shuffle their feet. "This is my friend."

"Of course. I suppose she's your brother's girlfriend."

Kylie smiled a deceptive smile, but it didn't deceive me. "Yes, she is."

I smiled at the newcomer. "Pleased to meet you. I hope you've brought Kylie's brother's VF Two. I'd love to see it. If the weather gets hot later, I hope it doesn't have vinyl seats. They'll burn your bum, for sure."

Kylie turned to her friend, who seemed lost, flummoxed. Maybe this one didn't speak any English at all. Kylie held up a slender hand to the brunette, then skipped to the bookshelf, grabbed the dictionary, and handed it to the woman. Like Kylie, she flicked through it, then turned to me. "I hope it won't burn me, but thank you for your concern."

Wait a minute. Were they learning to speak English from the dictionary? Was that why they'd both flicked through it and become the most articulate people you could ever meet? I sighed, too weary to pursue the thought. "So, what's your name, dear?"

Kylie muttered something that sounded like "wind," and the other woman seemed to have a basketball stuck in her throat. Her head jutted forward, her lips trying to form some word or other, and her throat rippled as though she had been struck dumb but was still trying to speak.

Kylie turned to her. "You can't say it here."

I'd had enough. "Why can't she say it? Did you say 'wind?' Oh no, please don't say Winona."

Kylie's face didn't betray any emotion at all. It would have been wonderful to watch, if it had been a comedy musical and not my bloody life. "It is. Winona."

I looked from one to the other, then back again. I must have looked like those clown heads that rotate from side to side with their mouths open as people try to throw balls down their throats at the funfair. "Okay, this has gone far enough. What's going on?" I had said, "This has gone far enough," at least twenty-four hours too late.

Kylie took a breath, but Winona... The other woman laid a hand on her arm. "You can't say."

"Yes she can, young lady, and she will, right now, or you

can both get out of my house." The shock had pushed my hangover to one side for a moment, but it wasn't ready to go without a fight, and my stomach boiled. "Excuse me." I ran to the bathroom. I made it, just. I heard Kylie shout to ask if I was all right. I hope she didn't hear my reply. Based on the last twenty-four hours, I felt sure she wouldn't have heard those words before.

8

I showed Kylie how to make tea and left her to it while I ratted through my clothes for some more old things I could lend to the naked stranger in my lounge. They owed me an explanation, but I didn't want to stare at a nude woman while they gave it to me.

I might as well have left her naked. They clammed up like the bad guys in the movies. Nothing. I've interviewed taxpayers and taxation inspectors alike, and I like to think I can see the difference between truth and lies, pretty good at getting to the core of any issue. I couldn't get a thing out of them except a cup of horrible tea I could barely drink. Kylie needed more training, it seemed.

I wasted an hour on questions, but they batted them off like a last wicket stand trying to eke out a draw with an entire session to play. Kylie had met Winona—I cringed every time I said or heard it—in the front yard as she came back from her walk. Winona had come to find out where Kylie had got to, but no explanation ever arrived about why their clothes had decided not to come with her. There was no Commodore, VF Two or any other model, and, as far as I could work out, no brother either. If they were playing truth or dare, they were the worst players in the history of terrible players.

In the end, I had a choice between two actions, each as bad as the other. I could kick them out of the house, despite my absolute certainty they didn't know shit from Shinola and would almost certainly end up in danger or trouble, or I could let them stay overnight, then drive them out to Lake George—I couldn't say "home" anymore, because I doubted it was their home—tomorrow. I'd wasted so much of the day asleep, quizzing the women, then trying to decide what to do, evening had drawn on, and I didn't want to drive back in the dark. I'm not afraid or anything, I just don't like driving in the dark.

When I told them they had one night before I kicked them to the kerb, Kylie became excited and told Winona about aloo gobi and wine, which I found a bit presumptuous. Kylie's enthusiasm for it became infectious, it seemed, and Winona wanted to try it. Wouldn't you know it? Another woman who's never eaten curry or drunk wine. What are the chances?

As I stood over the meal in the kitchen, I tried to come up with some rational explanation for everything that had happened. I couldn't find many rational explanations for it all. In fact, there were precisely zero rational explanations, which left me more than a little disappointed.

That left me with irrational explanations. I'd come up with one already: spacewomen. I rejected that. They both sounded as true-blue Aussie as you like, and they were human women, and how. Could they have escaped from an insane asylum?

Possible, but that would surely be on the news, and I'd turned the television on to rule that idea in or out. Out, it seemed.

I might have died and gone to some dystopian hellscape where naked women were my punishment until the end of time. If I kept accruing one a day, they would drive me crazy inside a week, and in any case, I doubted there was any level of hell that had Jo's silences in it. That's just taking things too far, so I ruled death out as well.

The aloo gobi didn't give me time to find an irrational explanation I liked, and I had to settle for small talk about how to cook it as both women gushed over how much they adored it. Then we all drank wine for a while. I didn't want another morning like the one I'd endured earlier, but, as I soon learned, doubling the number of naked women with no plausible life story lends itself well to consuming vast quantities of wine, and the evening became more jovial, if more unhinged at the same time.

Around nine, my phone rang. It wasn't Jo, and I wouldn't have answered it if it had been. She never liked to talk to me when I'd been on the grog because she blamed her father's death on that. It was the woman I regarded as my closest friend, Lucille. Not Lucy; Lucille. She was very insistent on that. It meant "light," apparently. Lucille was trans. I'd employed her some years earlier, before she committed to her change. When she said she wanted to transition and asked if she could keep her job, I said of course. She was an excellent accountant and one of those mythical good people, and she and I became friends as she looked to me for guidance in her new persona.

The global giant laid her off when they took us over. That's my biggest regret in the sale of the business, but to my delight, she soon found work with a smaller firm in Tuggeranong.

Maybe that had been the sub-conscious reason I lied to Jo about Kylie being from Tuggers. Lucille wanted to meet for coffee in the city on Saturday. I hadn't seen her for a while, and she was a lot of fun, which I felt I would need by the weekend, so I agreed.

That gave me thirty-six hours to move these two on. Tomorrow morning, I would drive them out to Lake George and drop them at whatever address they could come up with in the meantime. They would no longer be my responsibility, and I could get back to my usual, dull routine.

Routine. That reminded me of Rick. I'd met Rick about three months ago at the Labor Club. I'd gone there for a night out with a couple of friends, and we'd got talking. He invited me out to dinner, and we'd seen each other a few times. He was okay, too old for me really, even at fifty-seven. If ever a man had been old-fashioned before he'd been born, it was Rick. But boy, was he persistent. I told him right away I didn't want to get into anything serious, but after a month, he went all moon-spoon-June on me, so I stopped seeing him. He wouldn't give up, and after a couple of weeks, he talked me round.

We had a few more nights out, nothing more intimate than a few kisses in the car, but nothing about it worked for me, so I stopped seeing him again. He'd been calling again lately, begging for another chance, so last weekend I'd relented and gone to the movies with him. I agreed I might see him again, but the on-and-off thing was already getting boring, like a routine. He'd probably call tomorrow and try to persuade me to do something with him on Saturday night. Maybe I'd let him take me out and buy me a nice meal and a lot of wine. I'd earned it with these two. We'd see.

I woke on Friday morning in better shape than I had been

the day before. When I wandered out to put the jug on for a cup of tea, they were already up, sitting together on the lounge in earnest conversation. I didn't want to pry…

To hell with it. I did want to pry, but old mores nagged at me and told me to mind my own business. I muttered a good morning to them as I passed, but they didn't seem to hear. I stood at the counter and watched them, huddled together as they whispered to each other. The conversation looked intense, with a great deal of hand waving and occasional dramatic open-mouthed reaction, mainly from Kylie. Heads were shaken, hair flew around like a tornado in a candy floss factory, and at one point, Winona—groan—took both Kylie's hands in her own and whispered some firm words that required several sharp nods of her head as reinforcement.

I didn't want to call them Kylie and Winona, but the only other solution would be to call them Woman One and Woman Two, since they wouldn't reveal their real names. Things were weird enough without top secret experiment naming conventions, but inspiration struck, and I realised I could get their attention without recourse to their "names."

"Good morning, you two." I raised my voice, determined to make them hear me, and they both jumped as if they had been startled. It seemed they hadn't heard me arrive, boil the jug, cough indiscreetly, and drop a teaspoon onto the bench with a clatter.

Both heads swivelled toward me. Kylie reacted with a smile, Winona with a frown. Ho hum. At least I knew where I stood with the woman who had accepted my clothes, food, wine, and spare bed. It was an older bed and not as nice as the one in Jo's old room, so maybe she'd had a bad night and was just grumpy. Or maybe she was a miserable trout. Who knew?

Kylie's smile spoke a friendly greeting. "Good morning Abi. How do you feel?"

"Good, thank you. Would you like some breakfast?"

Kylie flicked her gaze to Winona, who didn't meet it and didn't respond. "That would be nice, thank you." At least Kylie had some manners.

"Does your friend eat animals?" I resolved to avoid the name Winona as much as I could.

"No, she feels the same way I do."

"I'll make some toast, perhaps. With peanut butter. It's plant-based. It's a good source of energy. Maybe she'll feel strong enough afterwards to say something."

Miaow. I could scratch and bite if I was pushed too far, but it didn't last. I already felt guilty about the sarcasm. I needed Jo to back me up, but that could turn into a physical fight, so it was for the best she wasn't here. Jo did not suffer fools gladly.

"That sounds nice." Kylie nodded her head as though to confirm the peanut butter on toast sounded like a feast fit for the Queen herself.

Winona's eyes narrowed, like Clint Eastwood's in The Good, The Bad, And The Ugly, in the gunfight scene. "I apologise if I seem rude, but our conversation is important."

"Winona, lovely, what could sound rude about that answer? It had been a model of social grace and self-awareness." I sighed and controlled my temper. I even stopped my foot tapping, my favourite sign of impatience. I threw out a magnanimous, sweeping gesture. "Please, continue your conversation while I make you some breakfast. After that, you can both take a shower, then I'll drive you home. Sound like a plan?"

Jo would have been proud of that. Assertive, confident, clear expectations outlined in an unambiguous way. Perfection.

On the subject of perfection, their perfect mouths both twisted in a way that suggested some element of my plan didn't meet their vision, and Kylie sucked in a short, sharp breath before she replied. "I don't think we need a shower." Something in her eyes at that moment reminded me of the look she gave me when she heard Jo suggest I should take her to the cops. Fear, or reluctance, at least. Who could be afraid of a shower?

Winona's crooked mouth, however, was for a different reason. "We'd like to talk to you about something before you drive us home." Her eyes darted to Kylie, then back to me. Suspicious and alarming. I don't like people whose eyes dart about when they're talking. Darting eyes usually mean hidden agendas, I've found. "We may not want to go home today. There's something we need to resolve first."

I tapped my foot on the kitchen floor.

9

Winona stared at me, but Kylie looked embarrassed, and she said nothing. The silence stretched on, and I wasn't sure who should break it. Me, I presumed. "What do you need to resolve?"

Winona's face remained stony, unreadable. "I'm afraid we can't say."

I hoped my face looked the same as Winona's. "You do realise you are guests in my house, I presume. I don't want to be rude, but what if it doesn't suit me for you to stay any longer?"

Kylie drew in a breath as though to speak, but Winona raised a hand that silenced her. The atmosphere had turned distinctly un-toast-and-peanut-buttery, and Winona's reply did nothing to take the chill out of the room. "That would be a nuisance."

If this was a tennis-like back-and-forth, it wasn't a friendly. We were playing for the claret jug, or whatever it is at Wimbledon. Claret jug might be golf. Mike played a bit of golf, and I think he told me about the jug once. Rats. *"Stay focused, Abi."*

I aimed for sardonic when I snorted, but I spat onto the bench, which minimised the impact and may have weakened my position. Advantage Winona. I had to take the next point. "A nuisance? That's an interesting choice of words." Not my best return of serve. I'd have to hope for a bad call from the line judges.

Kylie seemed to summon up some gumption. "Abi, I apologise. We have been rude and inconsiderate. You have already done so much for us, and it's an imposition to ask for more and take advantage of your kind disposition, but I promise we can explain soon." She flicked her eyes to Winona's dark, stormy face. They didn't linger, and I didn't blame them.

Damn. No help from the line judge. Kylie had made sure of that. I'd lost the point and the game, but I wasn't out of the set yet. My serve, and it had to be an ace. "I'll make us some toast." Damn, damn, damn. Double fault.

Winona stood, and I took a step backwards. I could see no point in the step, because the counter was between us, and she was at least three metres away, but in that moment, I did wonder whether she might attack me. "We'll finish our conversation in the bedroom, if you don't mind. Kylie will bring the toast."

Stevie Wonder could have seen the dynamic between them, but as soon as I thought it, I felt guilty in case I'd been rude to people with impaired vision. I took the bread out of the cupboard, then pulled the peanut butter jar after it as Winona disappeared into Jo's old room. Kylie hovered near the counter, uncomfortable, twitchy. She chewed at the inside of her mouth. As we waited for the toast to pop, I tried to lift the mood.

"Peanut butter is okay for you to eat. It's not real butter, just peanuts and a bit of salt."

"Thank you for being so considerate."

"This must be a very important thing you two need to resolve."

"It is."

I've never knitted fog. In fact, I've never knitted. It just wasn't my thing. But if I could knit, then knitting fog would have been easier than this stilted, awkward conversation. "She's very... Forceful."

"I'm sorry."

The Return Of The Two Word Woman. If that movie didn't already exist, we were in auditions for it. "What's going on, Kylie?"

Her sigh threatened my frosty exterior, like the times Jo got in trouble at school but refused to dob anybody in. She would take the blame, as though she was a member of a gang with a strict "no snitching" rule. Kylie seemed to want to tell me whatever they had debated earlier, but Winona must have told her what happens to snitches out in the Lake George Badlands. "I wish I could tell you. I hope I will be allow... able to tell you at some point."

I liked her, despite all the bizarreness that came with her. Meeting her had been like buying a lost suitcase from the airlines. You liked the case by itself, and when you opened it, there were all these odd things inside: other people's smelly underwear, strange plaster knick-knacks they'd bought in Bali or Honolulu, half-empty tiny bottles of shampoo or moisturiser they'd stolen from their hotel. I gave her my most hopeful smile and hoped against hope she wasn't in any kind of trouble. "Don't worry about it. I understand."

I didn't understand, not one thing about all that had happened in the last forty-eight hours. Good people can tell lies now and again though, and it doesn't make them bad people, just people who see someone who needs to hear something that will reassure them. Maybe my own reassurance would come along soon. I'd be on track to drink my wine fridge empty otherwise.

I spread the PB on the toast. I wanted to put as little as possible on Winona's, just a scrape that would barely register on her taste buds, but I worried she would make Kylie eat my pettiness, so I spread so much butter on the toast, it doubled the thickness of the bread. I handed the plates to Kylie with a smile. She returned it with a small, nervous thing that barely creased her magnificent cheeks.

I sat on the lounge and ate my toast, then had a bowl of cereal with too much milk just to spite Winona. *What do you think of that, then? I'm guzzling your precious animals here.* Cows have gorgeous eyes, and an image of a sweet jersey cow popped into my head. I hated myself for several seconds.

To distract myself, I picked up my iPad and scrolled through the news. That cheered me up so much, nothing could ever make me miserable again. The COVID situation was improving, but more than six million people had died from it. Russia's invasion of Ukraine continued, displacing millions. One of the British royal family had settled a sex trafficking case out of court. Madeleine Albright had died. Taylor Hawkins had died. Bugger. I liked the Foo Fighters. Will Smith had slapped Chris Rock at the Oscars.

I put the iPad down. So much for the world in the last few days since I'd taken any notice of it. The women were still in the bedroom, so I tidied some stuff up. When I say tidied up, I mean moved it from one inappropriate location to another, like dirty dishes from the counter to the dishwasher, or the borrowed shoes Kylie had left near the television to behind the lounge where I couldn't see them as easily. I picked up the iPad again and ballsed up a game of Sudoku so badly, I swore at it as though it had been the game's fault.

At last, they came out of the bedroom. Kylie sat in a chair, but Winona stood nearby. Kylie looked apologetic, her cheeks red, as she rubbed the fingers of one hand with those of the other. "Is it possible for us to stay another day or two please? I know it's a nuisance." Nice one, Kylie. She'd betrayed her doubles partner with a deliberate mishit.

I sucked at my top lip, something I've always done when I'm deep in thought. Not that deep, really, if I'm honest. How could I decide when I knew so little about why they'd asked? "Can you tell me why?"

Kylie drummed her fingertips on her thighs. "Winona has brought some news, and I need to decide what it means."

I looked at Winona from the corner of my eye when I answered. "Why does that mean Winona needs to stay? Can't she drive her boyfriend's Commodore back home?" I know they'd said the car wasn't here, but I needed to get back into the game before she annihilated me in an embarrassing shutout, leaving me red-faced and dejected at the press conference after the match.

Kylie sighed, a heavy, miserable sound in the tense room. "The news she brought me, I... I need to understand it more, and only she can help me."

"I see. This news can't be digested at home? Perhaps your brother could help you." I hadn't meant to be sarcastic to Kylie. I was guilty, but Winona was to blame.

"I may never be able to go home." The sadness in Kylie's voice speared into my heart like a... Well, like a spear, I suppose.

I watched her carefully. She didn't cry, but she looked more miserable than I'd seen her in the entire forty-eight hours I'd known her. "Are you in danger?" I had softened my tone, unable to maintain my anger in the face of her abject despair.

"I don't think so. I don't understand all the consequences of this news, if she is right."

Winona didn't waste a heartbeat to shoot Kylie down. "I am right."

I turned to Winona. "Are you a threat to her? I won't stand by and let you hurt her. I'd sooner throw you out into the street than see you do anything bad to her."

Winona studied me for some time, my unruly, uncombed hair, my tired Target sweatshirt, my favourite track pants, my overweight body. I resolved to do something about my weight, get back to where I used to be. I never wanted a woman I resented to sweep disdainful eyes over my too-robust figure again. The study went on too long, and I grew uncomfortable. As I battled with my choices—a discreet cough, or a cutting remark—she spoke at last. "You care for her. I see this, although you have known her such a short time. I have known her since..." She fell silent as she glanced at Kylie. "For a long time. No. I am no threat. I care for her also, but she has been misled, and I cannot allow that to continue any longer."

That explained everything. I saw it all now, as clear as day. No more confusion. The sun burst through the clouds of obfuscation and shone on us all with its benign countenance as it dispelled all misunderstandings and brought clarity to minds where previously only bewilderment had existed. "What the hell does that mean?"

I had her on the back foot now. Not much longer until we heard, "Game, set, and match, Mrs Lucas." Winona seemed to wilt before me, shredded by my astute insight, my brilliant repartee. "We can't tell you."

"For fu..." I cut off my profanity, frustrated as we circled back to where it all began. "For goodness' sake, Winona. Why should I help you if you won't trust me enough to tell me what's happening?"

Kylie's voice interrupted us. "Shall we go for a walk? I'm sure Winona would enjoy the view from Mount Painter."

The armies, thousands strong, in the war between Winona and me paused, as though they had cried aloud with one voice, "That's a good idea." I wasn't so sure and resolved to speak to their Captains later. "I suppose so. Some fresh air would be good. It mightn't be tainted with, 'Can't tell you,' and, 'Can we stay here?'" Sarcasm dripped from every word, and I felt proud of myself.

Winona had no shoes either, so I gave her a pair of Mike's, miles too big. I smiled inside and hoped she'd get a blister somewhere, possibly the size of a boil. Or even a tennis ball. Kylie walked in the middle, and Winona hovered so close to her, I wondered if the boyfriend/brother story had been made up because they were gay. That would stick it to men everywhere, if two such beautiful women only had eyes for each other.

I changed my line, a discreet alteration, and walked so close to Kylie, we bumped each other several times. Eat my socks, Winona. Two can play at this game. Maybe she'll choose me over you.

Why had I thought that? I shook my head and put some safe-as-houses heterosexual space between Kylie and me.

10

The wind seemed to dance around us, even though the trees barely moved over on Black Mountain. My untidy hair untidied around my face, while Kylie and Winona's streamed out behind them like a yellow and brown banner. We climbed to the top and sat on the rock again. I pushed strands of my hair, and theirs, out of my face non-stop. "What is with this wind?"

Neither of them spoke. Winona gazed up at the sky, and Kylie at the ground. A powerful gust threw grit into my face, and I turned my head to one side and scrunched my eyes closed. When I opened them again, Kylie nudged Winona, who looked around, then sat as still as death. The wind dropped, and so did their hair, which cascaded around their shoulders like security blankets. The strange thing was, it whistled around the pillars of the trig, but around us, it had turned as calm as you like, not a breath of breeze to tug at the least strand of hair.

I squinted at them. "That's not weird at all."

Winona tilted her head to one side. "Really? I thought you might find it very weird." The hint of a smile appeared at the corners of her full, red lips before she added. "I do."

"Did you have something to do with that?" I glared at her with all the menace I could muster, which probably wasn't much, if I'm honest.

She laughed. The first time I'd heard her laugh, I think. "That would be ridiculous." Her laughter continued.

I soon tired of the chortling. It wasn't even a funny comment, and I knew funny. I'd seen *The Princess Bride*, and I could laugh with the best of them, but this was other-worldly. "That's enough, for god's sake."

Kylie jumped in. "How could Winona have anything to do with the wind?"

The biggest fire starts with a tiny spark, and somewhere in the back of my mind, a spark flickered, tried for something flammable, then died out, alone and ignored. What had it been, that fleeting thought my brain had tried to latch onto? My mother always told me to let the thought go, and it would come back when it was good and ready. Experience had taught me that had been crap advice, but brooding on it would get me nowhere, so I pushed the whole tragic process from my thoughts.

To tell the truth, I enjoyed the calm. The wind had been bizarre and had driven me bonkers. We sat up there and watched other people come and go. We didn't say much, three women each lost in her own contemplations. Should I let them stay or kick them out? If it had just been Winona, I would have booted her, but Kylie seemed anxious and jittery, and I couldn't escape the thought she was at risk from something. I'd let Kylie stay a bit longer, but if that meant Winona stayed too, how did I feel about that?

Out of the blue, Winona reached out and touched Kylie. "You'd be okay in the shower, I think."

I gasped. "Why wouldn't she be?"

Kylie's mouth moved, but no words came out. Winona waited a moment before she answered. "She's afraid the water would be too hot."

My turn to laugh, and I did, raucously. An older couple with a small child—grandchild, I'd assumed—turned at the sound of my guffaws, and smiles spread to their faces. Amusement is infectious like that. I couldn't speak for a time as laughter shook me so hard, I thought I might fall off the rock and roll down the hillside to an inglorious end. "Too hot?" I squeezed the words out between peals of laughter.

Maybe humour is different out at Lake George, because they didn't seem to see the funny side of the foolish reply. It took me some time to calm down, and I didn't make much of an effort to spare their pride by rushing the process. When words would come at last, I suggested we should head home so Kylie could have her shower before the sun made the water even hotter. Another joke that landed on barren ground.

I jumped down from the rock, but I landed on a smaller stone—not a pebble, but not a rock either. My ankle twisted to one side, and I fell with a startled cry. The older couple ran over at once, all concern. "Are you all right?"

I wasn't. My ankle hurt, my pride had been bruised, and while she wasn't quite laughing, the corners of Winona's mouth twitched. Worse, neither of the women leapt to my aid, after all I'd put up with to help them. A tear trickled from my eye, maybe from the pain or the humiliation; I couldn't tell which.

The old man reached down to help me, so I grabbed his hand and heaved myself up. It wasn't my fault he was so frail, or that in my agony, I hadn't noticed. As soon as I pulled on his hand, he tumbled forward and landed on top of me. The old woman, his wife, I presumed, screamed and reached for him. For him, not me, even as all the breath in my lungs whooshed out of my mouth when his shoulder smacked into my stomach. He flailed about like a baby giraffe, all arms and legs and pathetic screeches.

Kylie seemed to realise something had gone horribly wrong, and she slid from the rock and reached for the old man. I wanted to scream at them, tell them they should be helping me, not him, the silly old fool. As he tried to right himself and scramble to his feet with the help of the old woman and Kylie, the old woman trod on my hair. The ankle forgotten, I screamed in pain and tried to extricate an arm to push her foot away, but she seemed to realise and moved it herself, delivering a swift kick to my ear in the process.

That had to be deliberate, some revenge for the perceived damage to her fragile old goat of a husband who didn't have the strength to lift a woman half his weight, or maybe a little more, without crashing down on top of her. The kid shouted, "Poppy," over and over, confirming the grandchild theory. What joy it brought me to be right about that in the middle of my distress.

Anyway, to hell with the kid. I saw stars after the woman kicked me, and the world spun before my eyes. At least Kylie and the woman had pulled the collapsed man off me, and I could breathe again. They helped him up and fussed around him, even when he assured them he was fine. I have never felt so relieved as when I realised he had taken no damage in an incident that had sprained my ankle, winded me, pulled half the hair out of my head, and concussed me so severely I would surely need a CAT scan within the next five minutes. I hoped the ambulance helicopter was already airborne. I might only have seconds left to live.

I whimpered, and Kylie seemed to remember I existed. She bent and looked at me. "Are you okay?"

"No, I'm not. She kicked me, and he winded me." That's when it hit me, that thought I'd been chasing for earlier. Wind. When Winona first appeared, I'm pretty sure Kylie introduced her as, "Wind."

Before I could pursue the thought to a conclusion, the old woman rounded on me. "You almost killed him."

I hadn't almost killed him at all, but I did almost punch her in the nose, even though I don't believe violence solves anything. Lucky for her she was standing up and I was lying down, or I would have extracted some revenge for the kick. "The old fool fell over. How is that my fault?"

"Well." She tossed her head as though I'd insulted her ancestors back to the dawn of time. "Some people."

Kylie placed a hand behind my head. "Can you sit up?"

I gave her a glum nod, and she supported my head as she helped me into a sitting position. The old man and his prickly wife moved off with the kid, who had started crying. I rubbed at my ankle, and Kylie glanced at it. "Is it okay?"

"I'm not sure. I hope so."

"She kicked you in the head?" I hoped my miserable nod conveyed the sense of indignity I felt at the couple's treatment of me. Kylie frowned, then held a finger up before my eyes. She waved it from side to side, and I knew the drill well enough to follow it. "You might have a mild concussion."

Mild? I was at death's door. What did Kylie know? I

huffed. I'd played victim enough. I'd birthed a child, for god's sake. I wasn't going to let a little fall and a kick in the head stop me. "I'll be right. Just help me up and let's see how bad the ankle is."

It hurt, but I didn't think I'd done any serious damage. Winona hadn't moved throughout. She sat on the rock, a slight smirk on her face. I tried to ignore her as Kylie draped one of my arms around her shoulders, like I had done for her two days before. We walked a few steps. The ankle felt tender, but I thought I'd be okay, although Kylie offered to help me if I needed it.

I jerked my head towards Winona. "Why didn't she help? Does she hate me or something?"

Kylie drew in a breath as if to answer, then flicked her eyes to Winona. "No, she doesn't hate you. She doesn't trust you, and she's busy anyway."

These days, when I frowned, I could feel my forehead touch my eyelids. I must do something about my weight. "Busy with what? And why doesn't she trust me? I've bent over backwards to help you both."

With another sly glance at Winona, Kylie led me a little further away, still with my arm round her shoulder as though we were testing the strength of my ankle. "I can't tell you much, not yet, but she's very important and has a lot to think about at the moment."

"Poor baby." There I went again, just thinking something but ending up with the words pouring out of my mouth.

Kylie either didn't understand sarcasm or took me at my word. "Well, we'll talk more about it soon, I'm sure. Meanwhile, let's get you home and get some ice on that ankle."

When did she become a bloody nurse? She knew nothing

two days ago, now here she was talking like a brain surgeon, expert in matters of the head and ankle. The sad part is I knew she was right. I had to read that encyclopaedia again and learn its secrets. She hadn't showered for two days, but she smelled wonderful, like apples and summer days and childhood dreams and... Woah. I shook my head. Where did that come from? I prayed to every god I didn't believe in I had only thought that and hadn't blurted it out. Kylie said nothing, so I might have got away with it.

We took a couple of steps, then Kylie turned and called to Winona, who slid from the rock and followed us in silence. It's pretty steep near the top of Mount Painter, but there are steps cut into the hillside, and with Kylie's help, I got down to the flatter part, where the path was wide enough for vehicles. I took a few tentative steps while Kylie fluttered, nervous, beside me, but I could bear my weight and only had a hint of a limp. I'd been lucky, it seemed; no serious damage.

Thanks to my stubbornness, we made it home without any further incident, and I let Kylie help me onto the lounge. She offered to make a cup of tea, and despite my misgivings, I accepted and gushed some thanks. Her skills hadn't improved, but it was warm and wet. The jug had taken care of the warm, Kylie hadn't buggered up the wet, but she'd done something to the taste I couldn't find words for. Perhaps there would be clues in the afterlife, but for now, I drank it with as few groans of horror as I could manage. I'd teach her how to make it properly another time. It felt good to have someone fuss after me. I'd grown unused to it these last two years.

"Snap out of it, you big baby." I snapped out of it. In a couple of days, they'd be gone, so no point in getting used to the thought of someone making my tea, even if it did taste as

though she'd strained it through a marathon runner's underwear.

Kylie sat on the edge of the lounge cushion, near my feet. "Will we have aloo gobi again? We both like it very much."

Winona seemed more present, and she nodded at Kylie's assertion. I remembered my thought up on the hill about wind. I'd come back to that. "There are other things we can eat. Aloo gobi gets a bit boring after a while, don't you think?"

"No, I don't think so." Kylie looked so earnest, I almost laughed. "It's delicious."

"We could have something else tonight but." I was sick of aloo gobi, despite her love for it. "I know you don't eat animals, but does that include fish?"

Kylie's eyes widened, the size of saucers. I'd never seen such big eyes, not even on cows. "I do not. If I ever had to eat any animal, a fish would be the last thing I would choose."

Her eyes watered, and she looked so upset, I stroked her arm. "Okay, we'll have something else. No fish." Why was she so attached to fish? Why did anything either of them did surprise me? They were the strangest people I'd ever encountered.

I asked Kylie to bring me a recipe book from the kitchen, and I leafed through it in search of vegetarian options. We settled on a lentil dhal, although I'd already grown tired of curries.

They wanted wine, but I said no, not tonight. They were drinking me out of house and home, and I felt bad about how much I'd drunk since they arrived. I fancied a glass after all I'd gone through today, but I told myself I couldn't rely on wine to carry me through the weirdness or I'd die from alcohol poisoning before they left.

I treated them to *The Princess Bride*, one of my favourite movies. They watched it, enraptured. Billy Crystal's Magic Max went over their heads, I think, but they roared with laughter at the sword fight between Inigo and Dread Pirate Roberts. They both looked shocked when it turned out Dread Pirate Roberts was really Westley, as though they'd been completely fooled by the mask. They exchanged awe-struck glances, and Kylie whispered, "Nooo," as Westley cried out, "As you wish," while tumbling down the hill.

When I woke the next morning, I had to make a decision. Should I cancel my coffee date with Lucille, or take the two millstones with me? Lucille deserved better than a last minute decision to abandon her, so I strode into the lounge and broke up their conversation about their oh-so-important revelations. "Get your glad rags on. Well, get some of mine on. We're going into the city."

11

They were much slimmer than me. That hadn't mattered in the slobabout trackie dacks and sweatshirts, but it did if I wanted to dress them up a bit. Even the clothes I couldn't fit into any more were big on them, but I didn't care. That was their own fault, truth be told. If they didn't want to wander around the country in the nude, they'd have to make do with whatever I had. I stifled a laugh at the sight of Kylie in one of my shirts. It was far too big and looked like a tent on her. Despite the unflattering clothes, she looked stunning.

I shook away the thought. I was jealous, nothing more, not that I'd ever looked like that, even in my best moments. We piled into the car, and to my surprise, Winona sat in the back. She looked scared to death of the car, and even Kylie didn't look comfortable, although she'd been in it already. They battled the seat belts until they were fitted, after a fashion, and we set off. Both of them stared out of the windows in awe, as though they'd never seen a building, a tree, or a Toyota Corolla before.

I parked in the Canberra Centre car park. Parking in the city centre, or Civic as we call it, is hell at the best of times, so I went straight to the mall car park. I turned off the engine and took a deep breath. Lucille was very much out and happy for people to know about her transition, and might mention it to the women. I worried about their reaction in public, so I decided it would be safest to let them know beforehand. "Before we get out, there's something I have to tell you. Lucille is trans."

In the mirror, Winona's face twisted into a back-to-front frown. "Trans is a prefix. Trans what?"

On a technical level, she was right. Transitive. Transform. Transmogrify, which I didn't know the meaning of, but I knew it was a word I'd heard somewhere. Trans had taken on its own meaning these days. Language changed and grew like a child, and here we had a classic example. "You're right, I suppose, but in this case it's become its own word. It's short for transgender. Someone who has changed the gender they identify as."

Beside me, Kylie mimicked Winona's frown, except hers was the right way round. "This is possible?"

I stiffened. Trans people copped a lot of abuse considering how few of them there were. Did these two have an issue with trans people? Did they believe the rubbish billionaire authors and the like were spouting these days? Lucille fit none of the stereotypes those people spewed out, didn't deserve the ugly treatment the haters dished out in the press whenever they got a chance. "Of course." Time to go into bat as an ally and a friend.

"I see." Kylie relaxed the frown. "If you're happy, so are we."

"It's not about being happy. It's about accepting people as they are and allowing them to identify however they want." I didn't know any of these things before Lucille decided to transition. Mike hadn't shared my views at first, but I didn't care. I'd refused to consider his fears about keeping her on at work and told him if he sacked her, he'd have to sack me. As my friendship with Lucille grew, I saw the utter hell she went through to become the person she deserved to be. Mike could take his judgement and shove it... I bit my metaphorical tongue. Nothing to be gained from speaking ill of the dead.

"Then let's have coffee with Lucille. I'm excited to try coffee. Is it like tea?" Kylie's face shone with an innocent enthusiasm, which must have made an interesting contrast with the darkness of confusion that spread through me, doubtless reflected in my own face. Another everyday thing they had no experience of. I must dig out the thesaurus when I got home; "Strange," wasn't cutting it anymore.

We got out of the car and walked through the Canberra Centre to the coffee shop I always met Lucille at, near one of the entrances to David Jones. Both women gazed about in wonder as we passed each store, often pulling one or the other to a window to peer at the displays, awestruck. If it had been possible to imagine, it would have been easy to believe they had never seen a shopping mall before.

On the drive, I'd told them the story I planned to use about them. I don't know why I had made up a story rather than trust to the truth. It may have been an aversion to having the authorities called to take me away for my own protection, put me somewhere quiet and safe where doctors could listen to my story of two naked women who had appeared in my life, neither of whom knew anything about the mundanity we took for granted, who learned the language from a dictionary they read in twenty seconds, and whom I had taken into my home against every sensible judgement any sane person could ever have made.

Lucille was late. Nothing new, sadly; you could set your watch by her arrival ten minutes after the agreed time, if watches still had minds of their own and weren't guided by some invisible clock in the ether that told them the time, accurate to the nanosecond and mindful of all the wacky daylight-saving ploys of humanity. We sat at a table and told the waiter one other would be arriving, and we would order then. The two faces opposite me wore bitter disappointment and impatience, but they would have to wait for their coffee. I tried to be more modern these days, but some old-fashioned ideas still stuck, one of which was never start to eat or drink until everybody can start.

She arrived, looking wonderful in a smart pair of trousers and a deep blue top. As always, her hair and makeup were impeccable. Coco Chanel herself could come back from the grave and dress me, arrange my hair and makeup, and Lucille would still outshine me in a pair of trackpants and a Mambo hoodie with a coffee stain on it. She had the confident swagger of someone who doesn't give two hoots what you think about her, and it radiated from her. She was lit from within, and the light that shone from her pushed back all the haters, the doubters, and the cynics.

I stood, we embraced and kissed each other, then I turned to the women. "This is Kylie and Winona." I gestured to each of them in turn, then to Lucille. "Lucille. Kylie and Winona are friends. Kylie is the daughter of a friend from Perth. They're doing a little tiki touring, and they're staying with me for a few days." Would Lucille understand tiki tour? I'd picked it up on a visit to New Zealand, liked it, and it had stuck.

Lucille smiled at them, a smile that welcomed them, trusted them as if she'd known them for years. They were with me, and if they were with me, they must be okay. "Lovely to meet you."

They both expressed similar sentiments, although Kylie managed to be more convincing than the ever-acidic Winona. Her face could curdle milk inside the cow. She had broken cover only when they watched *The Princess Bride*. At all other times, she was as miserable as the day is long. I commanded the uncharitable thought to leave, and it dragged its reluctant feet out of a mind that seemed unwilling to see it depart.

A young waiter came over, as though Lucille's arrival had freed his feet, which had been glued to the floor. I'd seen him hovering by the register eyeing Kylie and Winona. No doubt he couldn't wait to take their orders, impress them with his charm, perhaps try for a date or whatever youngsters called it these days. "Are you ready to order?"

I took the initiative to order espressos for Kylie and Winona, and a large flat white for me. No long blacks for them; if they'd never had coffee, I didn't want them bouncing off the walls for the rest of the day. He turned to Lucille, and his reaction told me he hadn't really noticed her until now, fixated on the two faultless examples of womanhood across the table from me.

I thought I saw a smirk on his face as he spoke to Lucille. "And for you, sir?"

Lucille ordered a flat white but didn't respond to his snide remark, and he walked off. I leaned close to her and whispered. "Lucille, why didn't you say something?"

Her smile looked genuine, but I saw enough hurt in her eyes to know the barb had wounded her. "It's nothing. He's probably never encountered anybody as fabulous as me and got flummoxed. Besides, I don't want to embarrass you or your friends."

Kylie switched her gaze between us as she tried to work out what had happened. It couldn't have been more obvious if she'd written her confusion up on a whiteboard. "What should Lucille have said something about?"

Winona leaned forward as I answered, similar bewilderment on her face. "He called her 'sir,' on purpose—"

"You don't know it was deliberate." Lucille interrupted me, prepared to give the man the benefit of the doubt, apparently not as angry as me.

I turned to her, stared into her eyes. "Of course it was. He thinks he's so funny..." I saw him carrying a jug of water and four glasses towards us, and I stopped.

He put the jug on the table next to the glasses and turned to leave. Kylie looked up at him. "Excuse me."

I tensed. They had no idea of protocol. I was livid, but it was Lucille who had been insulted, not me, so if she didn't want to make a scene, I would let it go. "It's okay, Kylie." I tried to head her off at the pass. It worked about as well as it works in the old cowboy movies.

"You called our friend, 'sir.' That's the wrong noun."

His eyes flicked to Lucille. "I apologise, madam." The smirk came back. He hadn't meant his apology, the little... He was sorry, sure. Sorry he'd been caught and called out on it.

Lucille nodded her head at him, done with the entire

episode, I guessed, but Kylie hadn't finished with him, to my disappointment. "Can we have another jug of water?"

He looked surprised. She hadn't said, "Please," which might have upset him. Poor thing. "This one is full." He gestured at the jug, which, as he had pointed out, remained untouched. Kylie picked it up, held it to her rosy red lips, and skulled the water in a heartbeat. Whenever I drank water that fast, I got a pain in my chest that suggested it had hit a blocked pipe and was about to burst out of my sternum in a flood, perhaps of Noah-esque proportions. Not Kylie. She sighed in satisfaction and held the empty jug out towards the astonished man. He stared at her as though he had been turned to a pillar of salt, and I blinked at my use of two bible references in quick succession. Pretty decent for an atheist. Kylie wiggled the jug in her hand and produced a flattering smile so powerful, I thought it might knock him to the floor.

He snapped out of his stupor, repaid the smile with one that, luckily, didn't shower Kylie in cheese, took the jug, and strutted away. Lucille broke the stunned silence at the table. "How long are you girls in Canberra for?"

I clenched my teeth. I'd briefed them, but they were like cats, unpredictable, bound to no fate but the one they were about to create for themselves and everyone around them. To my surprise, and relief, Winona found a smile from somewhere. Perhaps she had been watching us all and had finally mastered the art of imitation. "A day or two, I think. No more."

I didn't miss the look Kylie gave Winona, but she hid it almost straight away as Lucille replied. "You must get Abi to take you to the National Museum. It's fascinating."

Before I could reply, Kylie turned her head, and I followed her gaze. I swear the waiter's feet never touched the ground. He danced towards us like Patrick Swayze in Dirty Dancing. From the corner of my eye, Kylie sat rigid as she watched him. He reached the table, and at that moment, the water in the jug leapt out and dived straight at his groin. I couldn't find any other way to describe it. He didn't tip the jug, but the water spilled out, nevertheless. His pants took the entire jugful, and the stain looked as though he had suffered a tragic episode of incontinence. He held the jug away from himself and arched his upper body forwards as though it would save him, but when he looked down in horror, the evidence pointed to one thing, unless the moment had been observed.

"Oops." Kylie laughed as she said it, and I snorted. Lucille burst into uncontrollable laughter, and the waiter's face turned redder than any face I'd ever seen, redder than a face had a right to be. His veins stood out at his temple, his eyes were like saucers, and his mouth was wide open in a stifled cry of dismay. He slammed the jug down on the table, and water sloshed from it onto his groin again. I frowned. The jug had been emptied the first time. Where had this water come from?

Heads turned as the jug slammed onto the table. The young fellow mopped at his groin with the little cloth he carried tucked into the waistband of his pants, then turned and scurried away. Several of the other patrons watched him and sniggered or pointed him out to their companions.

As our laughter subsided, other than Winona, who had remained stony-faced throughout, Lucille turned to me. "Where did the extra water come from? I thought he had spilled it all over himself the first time."

Daughters can be a trial, and Jo had vexed me so many times in my life, I had often wanted to trade her in for a better model, but she came to my rescue at that moment. The dulcet tones of Christopher Cross rang out across the café, and I gratefully pulled the phone out of my bag. "Hello, darling." I don't think I've ever gushed at her so much since her father died. I had no explanation for what had happened, so I was happy to duck out, chatter to Jo for a moment, and hope Lucille forgot about it.

Jo wanted to catch up for breakfast in the morning and wouldn't take no for an answer. "I have the women staying here still."

My ears rang from the particularly virulent silence. "Women? How many are there now?"

I collapsed inside. I hadn't spoken to her since Winona arrived, and I'd tripped myself up. Mike used to have a sign on his desk that said, "Ensure brain is engaged before operating mouth," and I had failed to do so. "Two."

"Two? Who's the other one?"

At least she'd spared me another silence, one small mercy to be grateful for. "Her friend."

"Does this friend have a name? A home? A car to drive the first one away in?"

"No car. They both live out there." I had to be careful not to say they lived at Lake George now I'd told Lucille they lived in Perth. I'd already dug a pretty deep hole, but somehow, I couldn't stop digging.

"What's going on, mum?" A softness had crept into her voice. "Are you okay?"

Poor Jo. It must seem weird. Poor Jo? Poor me, more like. I was right in the middle of it. I thanked the stars Jo hadn't seen the water business. "Where shall we meet for breakfast?"

"Don't change the subject."

"Jo, I'm with Lucille. We're having coffee, so I can't really talk. We'll talk tomorrow. Just tell me where and when."

Jo picked a café near Lake Ginninderra, we said goodbye, and we left a lot unsaid. Lucille had been talking to Kylie and Winona while I'd been on the phone, and she didn't return to the question of the water. We enjoyed coffee and cake and a good long chat before we parted with more hugs and kisses. Winona seemed uncomfortable with the hug, but once you were in Lucille's inner circle, hugs were obligatory.

On the drive home, Kylie wanted to know more about Lucille's transition. It wasn't my story to tell, but I told her in general terms what was involved, and she said she admired Lucille's courage to endure all she had gone through.

Winona asked about the peculiar signs painted on the road whenever two lanes merged into one. "Why does it say, "Lane one form?"

"It doesn't. It says form one lane."

She sucked in a doubtful breath. "Your words usually flow from top to bottom when they're written. This seems wrong to me."

I laughed. "You're not the first to think that. Back in the day, people used to paint a P and a T on the road, so it said, "Planet one form.""

Kylie stared at me. "Why?"

"Canberra." To any Canberran, that was answer enough, and that was all they were getting on "Lane one form" for today. I had so many other things I wanted to say, but I kept a lid on it. I'd get to it once we were home.

People call Canberra the fifteen-minute city because you can drive to most suburbs from another in fifteen minutes or less, and for now they had a fifteen-minute pass.

12

"Tea?"

If Kylie had intended to deflect me, it didn't work, even though she made tea so strong it could deflect a B-Double. "What happened in that café?"

"We met your friend and had a lovely time."

True, but that hadn't been my question. "And the water?"

She shrugged. "He was clumsy."

I let a derisive laugh loose in the room. "Clumsy? I saw the whole thing. It was as if..." I strove to get my ducks in a row in my head so they could only quack about one thing at a time. "It was as if the water had a mind of its own."

Kylie gave me the Stage One Frown, but the incident had warranted Stage Five at least, perhaps more. "Water has no mind of its own, silly."

I admired her reply, reluctantly. "How do you know? Did you read it in the encyclopaedia?"

She sucked in a long breath. "Abi—"

Winona interrupted. "No. Say nothing. You see what your little parlour trick did? I warned you about things like this."

Kylie rounded on her and spat angry words that took me aback. "Of course you did. You're so smart. What about yesterday?"

They had lost me. I'd been taken aback, and I needed to be afront. "Hold on. What are you two talking about? I've bent over backwards to help you." Not true, if I'm honest. My back probably couldn't have taken that, but I'd done plenty for them, they couldn't deny that much. "What the hell is going on? What have I invited into my home?"

Kylie still faced Winona, and I couldn't see whatever was in her eyes, her face. "Winona, Abi's right. We owe her an explanation."

Fury surged to Winona's face, and I took a physical step backwards. Now I really was aback, and getting afront again might have to wait until Winona calmed down. "We owe her nothing. We owe them nothing. I have told you what happened."

My metaphorical hackles rose. Humans don't have hackles, but I wished I had some at that moment. "'Them?' Who are, 'them?'"

Kylie turned to me, a terrible sadness in her eyes. "I want to tell you. You have been kind to me."

Winona grabbed Kylie's arm. "Do you forget who I am? I have told you to tell them nothing. Do you no longer reside in the Balance?"

I directed all my fury at Winona. "Don't you grab at her like that, and don't you speak to her like that, not in my house. I won't stand for it, do you hear me?"

Kylie placed her hands to her ears, like she had done that

first day. I'd raised my voice, but not that loud, I didn't think. Winona turned cold, soulless eyes to me. "You cannot tell me what to do. I am..." She seemed to think better of whatever she had been about to say, and she tossed the endless acres of brown hair on her head in a display impressive enough for a shampoo commercial. "You need know nothing of our business."

I folded my arms, an impotent gesture of a dominance I didn't feel. "Then you needn't stay in my house, need you? You are free to leave. Don't forget to leave my clothes behind."

My entire body shook like a tree in a storm, mostly from anger, but also partly from fear. Winona's words were strange and threatening, and I didn't know what she might be capable of.

Kylie sighed. "Winona, I'm going to tell her. As she says, you can stay or go, that is up to you, but I intend to be honest. I think she deserves it, even if you don't. I know you are a Guardian, but you aren't one of my Guardians. You can leave if you don't want to be part of this."

I closed my mouth and wiped the dribble from my chin myself. Kylie had already proved more than once she wouldn't help with that, and it was time to assert myself a little, I felt. "Who's 'she?' Something the cat dragged in?"

Kylie's eyes burned with bewilderment when she turned to me. "You have a cat?"

"No, I don't... It's an expression. It means you're talking about me as if I wasn't here. I've never had a cat, but Jo once asked for one." "*Shut up, Abi. You've just moved yourself about five abacks.*"

Winona's glare almost cut me in half, but I held my ground. They were guests in my house, and unless they behaved with a bit more respect, they could bugger off. "You don't know what you're talking about. If she"—she nodded her head towards Kylie—"says anything now, it risks a great deal."

"Risks what? I don't understand." I hoped my voice didn't convey the complete lack of comprehension I felt.

Winona gave her head one sharp nod. "I know you don't, and it would be best if you never did. She should have stuck to her task and not lingered to befriend you. Now she has created the risk she may not complete her task. She has forgotten she resides in the Balance."

Kylie tossed her hair, a weak effort compared to Winona's gold-medal performance earlier. "I reside in the Balance. So does Abi, which I think you forget. She is one of us and deserves to know."

I didn't count how many times I blinked. I might not even be able to count that high. *"Balance?" "One of us?"* The whole thing had passed beyond strange straight into farce. "You're both talking in riddles. Look, I've tried to help you, but something is going on, and you've ignored my attempts to get you to tell me about it. Either tell me whatever it is you want to say or get out. Both of you." The salt burn of tears threatened, but I fought them with all my might. I didn't want to appear as weak as I felt.

Kylie took one of my hands in hers. "Perhaps we'll forget the tea. I think you'll need some wine for all I have to say."

"Kylie—"

"No, Winona. I have heard you, but I have made my decision. After all, who knows if you or my Guardians are right? What if none of you are? I can't make that decision. In these forms, we are equal. I have been given my task, and I will complete it, but to visit all we have on Abi these past days without any explanation..." She sucked in a breath and shook her head. "This is not the Balance."

Winona glowered at Kylie for some time. You could have cut the atmosphere in the room with a knife, but I was glad nobody tried. Winona didn't seem as though she could be trusted with sharp implements at that moment. She shook her head. "Very well. I will remain to see how this turns out. I have warned you of the risks. If you do this, it is your decision to carry. I hope your Guardians understand when you arrive at the new water."

I slumped down onto the lounge. It had all got too much for me, and I felt faint. The room spun, and I could no longer trust my legs to hold me up. Kylie whipped her head around, concern in her eyes. She crouched in front of me. "Are you okay, Abi?" Her soft voice soothed me, but only for a heartbeat. All they had said since we got home swam through my head like a school of piranha determined to devour every morsel of my sanity.

I managed a weak nod as Winona folded herself into an armchair, her legs drawn up underneath her, her face set in resolute anger. Kylie wandered into the kitchen and returned with a bottle of wine and three glasses. I glanced at the clock. Not quite three o'clock; early, even by my recent standards, but I couldn't deny how much I needed a drink already. The heavy sensation in my heart told me I wouldn't enjoy whatever Kylie seemed about to reveal.

Once the glasses were full, Kylie scooted across the carpet and sat with her back against Winona's chair, as though she wanted some space between me and them. Perhaps she wanted the reassurance of Winona's closeness. Winona's eyes suggested Kylie's choice of location might have been unwise.

The statuesque blonde wouldn't see the knife that stabbed down into her and took her life.

I took a long pull of the wine, heaved in a long, stuttering breath, and fixed Kylie with the bravest stare I could manage. "Let's hear it, then."

13

Kylie never allowed her green eyes to wander away from mine. "I'm not sure how to start, to tell you the truth. I've never had to tell this story." She gave a soft laugh, as if she found it ironic that the moment had arrived and found her unprepared, like someone going on holiday who hasn't packed when the taxi arrives. "We do not come from this globe originally."

I held up a hand. We were one sentence in, and I already didn't believe her. "Globe?" Why had that been the part I'd questioned, when the entire sentence made zero sense?

"Planet, then. That seems to be the word for globe here. Once, long ages ago, we all existed on a different globe."

I sipped at my wine. "Are you taking this from a Star Trek episode?"

"I have never seen Star Trek."

I muttered. "Of course you haven't. Are you making it up, then?"

Kylie smiled, Winona glowered. Kylie spoke, Winona stayed silent. "Abi, this will take longer if you interrupt after everything I say."

I barked out a laugh; more a scoff, to tell the truth. "I'm sorry I'm trying to understand while you're telling me you're a spaceman. Woman."

"I see that, but try to listen and let the understanding follow."

"What are you now, some kind of motivational bullshit peddler?"

She shook her head. "No, it's just... I think you'll find this difficult to believe, but if you hear it all together, it might make more sense." I waved a hand at her to continue, topped up my glass. "We lived on our globe, and we were content. We tended the animals and resided in the Balance."

I'd failed already. "The Balance? What is that? You've mentioned it before."

Kylie glanced up at Winona as though in search of inspiration. Unlucky, kiddo. She turned back to me. "It is the Balance. You might think of it as the order of things, a state where everything is in harmony with everything else, where all actions work together to promote a state of existence. The Balance."

"Like Nirvana?"

She half-closed her eyes. "Not quite, but it will serve as a concept. The Balance is more than a place or a state of being. The Balance is completeness. We serve her when we reside in her."

"Her? It's a woman?"

Kylie chuckled. "I don't know whether I'm a terrible storyteller or you're terrible at doing what you're told." I held up two placatory hands and she went on. "The Balance is the only gendered thing on our globe. All else—the People, the Gods, the animals—are ungendered. This is why I found Lucille's situation so full of intrigue. I digress. We all thought we were content. The People were divided into three cohorts. Each had the responsibility to tend for the three sets of animals—those in the water, those in the air, and those on the ground."

"What type of animals? Cows, fish, birds, that sort of thing?" The whole tale beggared belief. This wasn't Star Trek, it was The Twilight Zone.

"The animals were not as they are here. Like us, they were..." She seemed to reach for the correct word. "Ethereal. Without form. Every cycle, we changed our environment to tend for a different set of animals. Water this cycle, air next cycle, and so on. We never stayed in one element beyond the next cycle. Life went—"

"How long is a cycle?" I couldn't help it. The story was fantastic, and not in a good way. I topped my glass up again. Was one of them drinking my wine on the quiet?

"I can't answer that. In your globe's time, I have no idea how long it might be. A minute or a thousand years. I don't know. I'm sorry." She seemed prepared to ignore the matter as she pressed on. "Although we thought all was well, it was not. The Gods had become discontent, and they fought among themselves."

Winona interrupted at that, and I looked up at her. Some rare sign of passion shone from her eyes. "That is not the truth."

Kylie craned her head around to look up at Winona. "It would be best if I recount the Histories as I understand them. You can correct the points you disagree with afterwards."

"Good for you, girl." "Why had they become unhappy?"

"The Histories do not say much about how it started. They all wanted to be associated with one element or the other, rather than all the elements. Such a state cannot be imagined. It would not be possible to reside in the Balance in this way, or so we thought. Their arguments grew so ferocious, they brought about the Great Catastrophe, a disturbance in the Balance so great, the Mantle tore."

I held up a hand again. "A great disturbance in the Force? This is Star Wars. You're taking all this from the movies. And really? 'The Great Catastrophe?' Who wrote that line, Dick Dastardly?"

Winona shook her head as Kylie answered. "That would be impossible. I haven't seen those movies. *The Princess Bride* is the only movie I've ever seen. I don't know anything about Dick Dastardly either."

"What's this Mantle, then?"

"It is the Mantle. You might call it space, I suppose. It is the Mantle, the place where all the globes exist in the Balance. As I say, the Mantle tore, and the People fell through the rend before it could repair itself." I squeezed my eyes shut in disbelief, but I resisted the urge to interrupt. "We fell for endless cycles until we came to this globe. This globe was strange to us, and we were afraid. We huddled together and looked to the Guardians, those among the People entrusted with the recollection of the Histories and with ensuring we all reside in the Balance. The Guardians tried to tend us on this unfamiliar globe, but the Gods continued to fight."

I stood up. The bottle was empty, and I stomped into the kitchen to grab a replacement. I stood at the sink and looked at the two women, who watched me in silence. I pinched my side, low down out of their sight, to make sure I wasn't just having a bad dream. It hurt, and disappointment washed over me. I looked at Kylie. "I didn't come down in the last shower, you know. I don't believe you. This is all rubbish. Why are you making up all this crap?"

14

Kylie smiled her beautiful smile. "Listen to me for a few minutes more, then decide. I ask it as a friend."

I thought that was a low blow, but for some reason I couldn't explain, I had grown fond of her, and although she had just spouted a cartload of poppycock, part of me wanted to believe her. It would explain some of the weirdness, at least. I snatched up the bottle from the counter and returned to the lounge.

"The Gods fought here, as they had on our own globe. In the end, the Guardians achieved some form of peace by agreeing to divide the People between the elements without any rotation through each one as the cycles passed. I chose water. Winona is a Guardian of the air. I have tended the animals in the water where you met me for endless cycles."

"What do you mean when you say you tend them?"

"We move around them, past them. It reassures them."

I shook my head as my brain exploded. How could I ever

get my head around such intangible concepts? I'd spent my adult life tallying numbers, where one column had to equal another or someone had made a mistake. These ideas were out of reach, no matter how I tried to snatch at them. "Reassures them how? What are they afraid of?"

"Everything. Nothing. It is our role. It is what we do to reside in the Balance. Most of the time, I don't know whether the animals on this globe even know we are there. They do not calm when I pass them if they are agitated, like when one of the Uprights disturbs the water."

"Uprights?"

"You call yourselves humans now, because your People have forgotten the Histories. You are us. You are the People who chose to tend the animals on the ground. You had to take this physical form because of the force that pulls us downwards."

I frowned as I tried to unravel the explanation. "Gravity?"

"I know it is gravity now, thanks to your books, but we could not understand it. It did not exist on our globe."

"So how come you didn't, you know, whizz off into space, or the Mantle, or whatever?"

"I cannot answer that question, but we didn't. The water you call Lake George was populated by our People many cycles ago, but it disappeared, and the People faded. Now the water is full again, and the Guardians want our People to populate it once more. I have been chosen to travel there and enter the lake. There, I will divide and re-populate the water. That is why I must reach it."

I leaned back and placed my hands behind my head. What a ludicrous story, but there had been some strange goings-on. "The water in the café?"

"I commanded it to do as it did. I can control the water, because I am of the water. Let us call my People the Dwellers, for ease."

"That's a sillier name than Uprights." There I went again, just thinking something but ending up saying it. "How did the jug get full again?"

She shrugged. "Water is everywhere. Your body is mostly water. I refilled the jug by commanding water to enter it. You didn't notice, Lucille didn't notice, and he didn't notice it, because I took a small amount from each of you."

I turned my attention to Winona. "The wind on Mount Painter?" She nodded. She had controlled the wind so it wouldn't blow on me? Who would believe this stuff? I drained my glass. "Prove it, each of you. Fill my glass with water, right here."

"I will not. I am a Guardian. I do not play stupid games at the request of Uprights." Winona folded her arms, further confirmation she wouldn't do what I asked.

Kylie sighed and sat still for a second, two at the most, and the wine glass filled with water. I stared at it in disbelief. "Where did that come from?"

"From us. I took some from each of us. Too small to notice, but enough to fill the glass."

I shook my head from side to side, unprepared to believe my eyes. "Impossible."

"Watch, then." Kylie knelt at the table and held her hand over the glass. The water flowed up and stopped, a column from her hand to the glass. She turned her hand over, and the column pointed from her palm to the ceiling. She flicked her hand, and the water splashed into my face, down my top. I spluttered and spat out some water from my mouth as Kylie laughed. Winona's countenance darkened. If her face turned any darker, she would be able to hide in a bucket of coal.

I wiped my face with my sleeve and refilled my glass with wine. "This is hard to believe."

Winona leaned forward. "It should be, because most of it isn't true. Her Guardians have told her falsehoods. Whether they have forgotten the Histories, or they work to some end the Gods require, I cannot guess. The Gods did not cause the Great Catastrophe. We did. We fought among ourselves over which element was best until the Mantle tore.

"When we reached this globe, the fights continued, and we became three separate people, each confined to our own element. That is why we cannot see each other. The Gods punished us for the rend in the Mantle, and we can no longer see each other."

I gasped. "You can't see her?"

"I can see her in this form. We are in Upright bodies and must obey the physical laws of this form. I see her, but I could not see her when she resided in the water. I knew her on our globe. She was destined to be a Guardian, diligent and devoted to the Balance. She tended the animals and loved them all, regardless of which element they existed in. Her name was..."

She fell silent and pulled some unattractive faces. I thought about taking a couple of photos, because nobody would believe how ugly those faces were without them if they saw her perfect cheekbones and... Never mind that.

Kylie spoke, soft, as if she was afraid. "For some reason, we cannot say our names here. That is why I could not answer when the man asked, and why I took the name you suggested."

"I didn't suggest it, exactly."

She ignored my feeble interruption. "That is why I

accepted Winona's name. I now understand why these names are so inappropriate. When I first met you, I couldn't speak your words, but I understood them as you spoke. I could answer you, but only with words you had used already. The dictionary solved that issue."

"Why do you cover your ears sometimes?"

"When I first heard your voice, it seemed loud to me. We do not speak. We think. It is called the Thought, or that is the best translation I can find for it, at least. The man had a very loud voice. It hurt my ears."

"Why were you so anxious when we reached the car?"

She blushed a little and laughed, one of those silly laughs you give when somebody has caught you being a dickhead. "I didn't realise it was a car. I thought it was one of your animals, and you were tearing it apart and pulling bits of its inside out."

Under different circumstances, that would have been stupid enough to make me laugh with her, but these weren't different circumstances. "And the cops?"

"I believed they might be your Guardians. I feared they might interrupt me in my task, so I didn't want to take the chance."

It made sense now, other than the parts that didn't make any sense at all, which was all of it. It was all mumbo-jumbo, if you ignored the fact she actually could control water with her mind.

Winona's voice made me jump, lost in my thoughts. "She is wrong also about the People in the water at Lake George. They did not fade. We cannot fade. We are immortal. They left the water in Upright form and now reside among you."

Kylie turned to her. "That is not true. Why would they not go back to their own water, if that was the case?"

"You've asked me this so many times. They are now Uprights. They have been Uprights for so long, they cannot remember when they lived in the water. Who knows what their new Guardians have told them? Perhaps they enjoy the Upright form."

"My Guardians told me once I re-entered the water, I could never receive the Kiss of the Gods again. I could never take Upright form again, ever."

"I don't believe that, although I have no evidence to prove or disprove it."

I'd only half-listened to their debate, because another thought gnawed at me. "We don't tend the animals. We eat them."

They both turned sad, haunted expressions my way. "You have forgotten the Histories and no longer reside in the Balance." Winona had dismissed the entire human race with such a simple phrase.

"One more thing." I felt sure I had them with this one. "If you can't see each other, why did you come here, to my house, after Kylie arrived?"

Winona didn't collapse into a bawling, wretched mess, begging for my forgiveness for the stupid story they'd made up. "I am a Guardian. I did see her, but she is not in her own form. She is in the form of something that has forsaken all our People stood for, even though she has not. Everywhere she went, she disturbed the Balance, and I knew from previous encounters what that meant. One of the Dwellers had taken Upright form. I had to understand why. That was when I discovered the untruths she had been told by her Guardians."

I felt pretty drunk, and more than half the second bottle had gone. I needed some food to mop up some of the alcohol. I couldn't face cooking, so we looked at the menu of one of the local Indian restaurants, and I ordered some food through Uber Eats. Kylie took her first sip of wine, but Winona showed no sign of drinking hers.

I sat with them, alone in my thoughts. How could I accept such a far-fetched tale? On the other hand, how could I ignore the tricks with the water, and the way Winona had stopped the wind, if she had, in fact, done that, and it hadn't been some quirk of nature she took credit for. I had no litmus test I could subject them to so I could determine the truth. If I had ever encountered alien beings before, I either hadn't noticed them or had been too drunk to remember it now. I cursed the coffee I'd bought on Wednesday morning. It had led me into this demented horror story, and I hadn't even had the pleasure of finishing it. I should have left Kylie to Mr Noseypants and his fleabag of a dog.

The ring of the doorbell startled me. Kylie answered the door and took the food from the driver, dished it out onto plates, and brought them into the lounge.

I stared in dejection at the food. "All of it? That's too much for us. You should have left some of it in the containers. We could have put it in the fridge and had it another day."

She looked downcast. "I'm sorry. I didn't think of that."

I took a mouthful of food and mumbled through it. "Forget it. I don't suppose the takeaway portions were this big on your planet."

We ate in silence until I felt fit to burst. I decided I could scoop what was left back into some of the containers and put it in the fridge. The wine bottle was empty, and so was I. The whole story had drained me. I'd run out of energy and the ability to believe anything they said. "I'm going to have an early night. I'm meeting Jo and her family for breakfast in the morning. If you're still here, I suppose you'll have to come with me." They said nothing. "Good night."

Kylie wished me a good night and hoped I slept well. Winona said nothing. Miserable trout.

15

I felt atrocious the next day, as I'd known I would. I'd drunk too much and eaten too much, and I hadn't put any of the leftovers in the fridge. I nursed my aching head and body through a shower, which made me feel no better, then wandered out to the lounge. They were both up already. "Don't you two ever sleep?"

Kylie looked up. "Yes, we do. We seem to wake before you though."

I went into the kitchen to make a cup of tea. They'd tidied up, at least, but when I opened the fridge, they'd put the three plates in there with the uncovered food still on them. I sighed. It was my fault. I should have put it back in the containers before I went to bed.

I took my tea to the lounge. "When you meet my daughter and family, don't do anything weird, okay? And for god's sake, don't mention any of that stuff you told me last night. Jo will have us all committed in a heartbeat."

"Committed?" Winona wrinkled her nose in confusion.

"Locked up. Sent to an asylum for the insane." Both were back in trackpants. "Have either of you showered since you arrived?"

Kylie nodded enthusiastically. "We have. I was afraid I might return to the water if I went into it, but I didn't."

That was something. There's nothing worse than disappearing down the drain of the shower and being spewed out into the nearest lake, in my experience. "What are your plans now?"

"We're coming with you for breakfast." Winona didn't crack a smile as she made the inane reply.

"I don't mean right now. I mean what are your plans as far as Lake George are concerned now you've told me this crazy story?"

Winona nodded as though all had become clear. "The water is none of my concern. That is a task given to"—she pulled the ugly faces for a moment, then seemed to give up—"Kylie."

"So what will you do?" I hoped she'd leave, and sooner rather than later. I was done with her moodiness.

"I know why she has assumed this form. My task is complete, and my People need me. I will Translate."

I wondered if I'd misheard. "Translate?"

"Yes. That is what we call it when we change form and move to a different element."

I stifled a laugh. "I don't think that's the right word."

Winona's angry eyes bored into me like two white-hot laser beams. "It is not for you to say whether our words are correct or not. That is the best equivalent I can find among your clumsy words."

I held up two fingers. "Translate that, bitch."

Kylie looked shocked. "That is a despicable insult. I don't like it."

"You'll get over it." I was in no mood to humour them or their fragile sensibilities. I glared at Winona. "When do you plan to Translate? What can I do to make it sooner?"

She flashed a vicious smile. "Who got out of the wrong bed this morning?"

I couldn't stifle the laughter this time. "I don't know where you learned that, but it's wrong side of the bed."

She seemed puzzled. "Are you sure?"

"Darling, I think I know our clumsy words a little better than you. It's wrong side of the bed."

"I will accept your correction, in that case."

I'd finished my tea and I was finished with her. "Are you going to change or go like that?"

Kylie stared at me. "We cannot Translate. They will not see us."

My smile didn't feel cynical enough, but in my defence, I had a hangover. "What a disappointment for them. I meant your clothes."

She nodded. "I see. We have no other clothes, and I sense you would be hostile to a request to borrow some of yours."

"What happened to yesterday's clothes?"

"They are in our rooms."

"Then put them on. Hurry now." I clapped my hands, but Kylie covered her ears. Too loud, I presumed. "Go and put those clothes on, and we'll head off."

We drove down to the town centre, and I parked on Emu Bank. Jo, Steve, and Grace had already taken a table, but we needed a second pulled over to accommodate all six of us. I introduced everybody and ignored Jo's razor-sharp stare. She had a talent for recognising the weakest member of the herd, and she turned straight to Winona. "Winona. Such an unusual name. Where are you from?"

I couldn't blame her for the reply. The story had changed so much, even I was confused by it all. "Perth."

Jo's uncanny ability to combine genuine interest and lethal disdain into one facial expression was probably unequalled. "Really? There's a Lake George in Perth as well?"

Winona's brief experience as a human hadn't equipped her for Jo. Let's face it, at forty-nine, I still struggled with her acerbic nature when she turned it on full blast. Winona looked at me, but I gave her a smile loaded with pretend sympathy. "You're on your own, I'm afraid."

Winona turned back to Jo. "I'm from Perth. She's from Lake George." She waved a hand at Kylie. I begrudged the respect for the answer, but it hadn't been bad in the circumstances.

Jo didn't even pause for breath, like the Terminator, relentless, unstoppable. "Tell me about your name. I've never met a Winona before."

"What a disappointment for the Winonas of the world." I looked down, or I swear I would have burst into laughter at Jo's face. I didn't begrudge the respect this time. Winona had taken my sarcasm from earlier and turned it on a thoroughly deserving Jo, and I didn't want to get in between them now they'd both turned up the heat.

I don't know whether Jo was speechless, but this silence wasn't the ones I'd grown used to. I risked a glance at Steve. He'd looked away too, but he wore his smile in his shoulders, which chuckled up and down as he battled the lols.

"Well, aren't you the spicy one?" I looked up in surprise. Jo had given up if that was all she had. Winona had beaten her, and it hadn't taken long. I couldn't believe it. Jo's red cheeks and the furnace in her eyes confirmed it. She was fuming, but she'd drawn a blank on a suitable response. Winona actually looked smug, though where she'd learned it from, I couldn't even begin to guess.

The waiter rescued Jo, and we ordered. Avocado on toast for the vegans, bacon and eggs for the Carnivore Crew, and scrambled eggs for Grace. While we waited, I noticed Grace seemed fascinated by Kylie, who had sat next to her. Grace reached out and ran a hand through the lowest reaches of Kylie's stunning blonde hair. Kylie turned and smiled, then glanced down at the piece of paper in front of the child. It was one of those colouring things cafés often have for kids. Kylie pointed to it. "Are you going to colour that in?"

"Will you help me?"

Kylie's eyes flicked up to me, and I responded with a tiny nod. "I'd love to. What is it?"

"It's a mermaid, like you."

Heads jerked up, and eyes stared at Kylie, then flicked to Grace. "Kylie isn't a mermaid, sweetheart." Jo sounded apologetic, but Kylie didn't seem bothered by the comment.

I was. What if Grace had some sixth sense? My granddaughter might be some kind of savant who could see other-worldly creatures around her. If she spilled the beans...

Steve stepped in. "She thinks you look like Ariel, I think."

Grace gave him a withering stare. "Silly Daddy. Ariel has red hair. She looks like Madison."

I laughed and gave Jo an accusatory stare. "Have you been forcing her to watch *Splash*?"

"She loves it." Jo's defence of her addiction to the movie came too fast, too defensive.

"Don't go outside the lines." Grace's stern order to Kylie as she handed her a crayon drew us back to the picture, and they both bent to their task. It was hard to say who enjoyed it the most, and whenever Kylie glanced up at me, she gave me a huge, beaming smile. It diffused my anger, and I felt pangs of guilt about how I'd spoken to the two of them earlier. I even tried to smile at Winona, but she just glowered at me suspiciously.

Steve insisted on paying for everybody's breakfast, and Jo suggested a walk along the foreshore of the lake. Kylie seemed hesitant, but she'd survived the shower. Unless she fell in, she'd be fine, I thought.

In my mind, I kicked myself. She'd be fine? Did I believe last night's concoction? Of course not. Who would? We walked down past the pub and along the path between the lake and the restaurants along that part of the foreshore. The warm morning sun felt pleasant on my face as I wandered along at the rear of the group. Grace and Kylie were already inseparable, and Grace had slipped her little hand into Kylie's. I couldn't understand it. Grace had always been slow to befriend anyone, although unlike her mother, she loved you forever once she accepted you, but this seemed next-level, as though she believed Kylie really was a mermaid and had decided to cling to her for as long as she could.

We'd reached the footbridge that took one part of the path past the Arts Centre when the tragedy I'd dreaded all morning struck. Not the tragedy I'd feared, however, that Jo would trip the women into some confession of the crazy fantasy they'd laid before me last night. This was a full-blown real tragedy.

Grace's fascination with animals had been evident from a very early age, and two ducks waddled away from her and Kylie, who were in front of everyone else. Grace broke free of Kylie's hand and chased them. I couldn't blame Kylie. She had no kids, didn't realise how quick they'll be gone when they dart off after daydreams and shadows, or ducks, in this case.

The ducks weren't secret ninja assassins from Winona and Kylie's world, but the man on the bike might as well have been. He'd come tearing down the other path from the street, and Grace ran in front of him. I don't know who screamed the loudest when he clattered into the tiny three-year-old and sent her skittering onto the ground. Me, I think. Kylie came a close second, to my surprise. Five adults rushed towards the child, who lay on the path and cried, the sort of cry that crushes your heart in a vice and squeezes every fatalistic thought you've ever had from it.

Jo picked her up, pulled her to her breast. She'd cut her legs and one of her hands, and had a nasty scrape on her forehead, but she seemed okay as Jo ran anxious hands over her limbs to check for fractures.

Steve whirled on the man as he picked himself up gingerly. "You bloody idiot. Why the hell were you going so fast? You could've killed her."

The cyclist stiffened. "She ran in front of me, mate. And I'm fine, by the way."

Jo looked up, still crouched with Grace squeezed against her. "You're blaming her? She's fucking three, you wanker."

I grimaced. Jo's language could make a shearer blush, and her face suggested murder by way of retribution wasn't out of the question at that moment.

Cycle man was having none of it. "Then keep her under

control. Why wasn't somebody holding her hand, or better yet, why wasn't she on a leash?"

Steve growled at him. "She's not a bloody dog, you twat."

When the comment about someone holding Grace flew out on the spit from the man's mouth, I glanced at Kylie, who had been holding her hand right before the man appeared. As still as a statue, she glared at the man.

That's when the gust of wind blew the man into the lake, and my heart stopped.

16

At that precise moment, renewed cries from Grace had dragged her parents' attention away from the man for a moment, so they may not have seen it happen. I knew at once how he'd been blown into the lake, and any doubts I had last night seemed misplaced, especially when the man's bike flew into the air and crashed to the ground a good fifty metres away.

I yelled something. It might have been, "Holy shit." It might have been the lyrics to "Born To Run" for all I knew; I just made a petrified sound and dashed to the edge of the lake. I could see him below the surface, but he wasn't coming up. *"Swim, you idiot. It's only shallow here."*

I reached into the water and grabbed one of his flailing arms, but I couldn't pull him up. I looked around at Kylie. She stood stationary, disinterested almost, like Winona had been on Mount Painter, and watched with a cold dispassion I couldn't understand. I screamed, "Steve. Help me."

He glanced at me but seemed confused. He looked around

as though he tried to find the bicyclist, then looked back to me, an empty shell where a strong helping hand ought to be. Shit. I went to Plan B. "Kylie." It had to be her holding him under the water. I don't know which scared me the most: that she might drown him in her anger, or that I'd just accepted every crazy word from last night as gospel.

She looked at me, but those hard eyes didn't soften. I screamed her name again, and from the corner of my eye, I saw Jo and Steve turn their attention to her. For a second, I thought she might let the stranger die, but she shrugged her shoulders and gave me a smile so cold it nearly turned me into a snowman. Woman.

Bicycle Man's head shot up from the water, and he grabbed at me with one hand, the edge of the path with the other as he spluttered and spat water out of his mouth. Steve snapped out of his trance and helped me pull the man out onto the path, where he lay panting with less dignity than a beached fish.

I shot words at him, desperate to get rid of him now. "Are you okay? You need to get yourself off home and have a shower. I'm not sure how clean that water is. God only knows why you jumped in like that."

"I didn't jump in." He gasped between every word as he sucked in drafts of air. "I couldn't get out. It was like the water was holding me down."

"Don't be silly." Had I said that too loud? Had my laugh sounded too nervous? "You've been watching too much Star Trek." Damn, why the hell had I said that?

He gazed around. "Where's my bike?"

I pointed at it. "Over there."

"Are you mad?" He rose to his knees. "Why have you moved it over there?"

Steve leapt in to save me, Sir Lancelot to my Guinevere. "We didn't move it mate. It must have rolled there when you mowed my daughter down."

The man seemed to remember the incident and the argument, but he seemed more contrite. Getting blown into a lake and held underwater by fish will do that to you, I imagine. "I'm sorry, mate. Is she all right?"

Jo snapped back at him. "Yes, no thanks to you. Some cuts and bruises, but she'll be okay when I get her home and clean her up."

"That's good. I'm really sorry. I didn't see her until it was too late."

His change of attitude seemed to take all the wind out of the sails of Steve's angry yacht. "Yeah, well maybe take it a bit slower next time, eh?"

I heaved a silent sigh of relief. I had been afraid it would come to blows, and Bicycle Man looked lean and muscular, while Steve had the paunch and flabby arms of a man who does something in IT that involved no more exercise than moving a mouse around and playing the occasional game of Fortnite.

Who needed a muscular warrior anyway when you had two women who could blow entire men into lakes and drown them, all by will power alone? I dragged a weary smile to my lips from wherever my easy-going nature had hidden itself for the last ten minutes. "All's well that ends well. That's a little too much excitement for one morning for me, I'm afraid. Come on, you two. Let's head home."

I ignored Jo's protests and the strange look on Steve's face as I marched off. To tell the truth, I wasn't happy about any of what had happened. I was worried about Grace, of course, but Jo had said she was fine. Above all, I had no stomach for the incident to deteriorate any further if either Kylie or Winona decided to join in the exchanges between Jo, Steve, and the cyclist. I'd ring Jo later and check in on little Grace, but she was a tough kid. She had to be, to put up with her mother.

I love my daughter, but she's a hard woman with a vicious streak as wide as the Nullarbor. I hoped Grace grew up with a little more empathy and a lot less sulphur and brimstone. I suppose it's my fault, the way Jo turned out. I hadn't always been there for her when it mattered, and when, in the depths of my misery and degradation, she took her father's side, I think a little piece of my love for her died for ever.

I shook the thought from my head as I stomped to the car. I glanced back at one point to check the women had followed me. It would have been embarrassing if they hadn't, but there they were, silent and perfect, like most of the time.

I drove home, and I can't deny the police station on Benjamin Way tempted me. I could drop them in the car park, go home, and forget I'd ever met them. Had it just been Winona, I might have, but something about Kylie made me want her to stick around for a bit. I consoled myself by muttering, "You'll never take me alive, copper."

I shook the thought about wanting Kylie to stick around from my head. In the house, I made tea for us all and we took our usual stations, ready for the interrogation they weren't avoiding. "What the hell, you two? You could have killed him."

Winona's acidic countenance softened, which put me on the back foot for a moment. "I had nothing to do with any of it."

I spluttered. "Who blew him into the lake, then?"

"Me." Kylie's timid response sounded thin and lonely in the air between us.

"How? I thought you were the water baby."

Winona shook her head. "I told her we can control all the elements, just like on our own globe. Today, she found out I had told her the truth."

"Why, Kylie? Why did you do that? You might have killed him." Had I already said that? I needed to get a grip on my emotions. I shook with anger and worry, and I clasped and unclasped my hands in frustration.

It seemed Ms OneWordAnswer had returned. "Anger."

I could understand that. It must have been a shock when Grace pulled away from her and ran under the bike wheel. I tried for a softer tone, less accusatory. "Don't blame yourself. You're not used to kids, and the little buggers can squirm away and take off like—"

Kylie interrupted me. "Not my anger. Yours. Jo's. Steve's." My face must have said something like, "WTAF?" because she carried on. "In this form, we obey all the physical laws of this globe. We also have all the emotional capacity of an Upright, but we don't know how to use it. I take my cues from you. I could feel the anger from the three of you, and from him, which surprised me. It drove me to do what I did."

Get the front door. She was an empath, like that woman on Star Trek, the Patrick Stewart ones? "What? You feed off our emotions?"

Her long hair flicked around when she shook her head, I noticed. "No. We are connected, and I feel what the Uprights around me feel. On our globe, we tend the animals and reassure them so they don't become affected by the emotions of others. We are all part of the Balance, and we all share it, if we reside in it. You have lost your connection because you have forgotten the Histories, but we haven't. I haven't."

On one hand, I found it hard to doubt some of the things

they'd told me last night, especially after the display at the lake. On the other, I didn't know whether I could buy into this, "Kumbaya, we're all part of one great ball of energy," stuff. I decided attack was the better form of defence. "You might have drowned him."

"He would not have drowned. I made sure he had enough oxygen. Murder is a crime on your globe."

"It isn't on yours?"

"It doesn't exist on ours."

Smug cow. "How did you make sure he had enough oxygen?" The air quotes I air quoted were so vicious, they could have cut paper. Quite thick paper.

She shrugged. I hate it when people shrug me off. "Water is part oxygen. I made sure only the oxygen entered his lungs every time he swallowed water."

I closed my eyes, more of a squint of WTF-ishness really, I suppose. "You called the water out of him like some sort of exorcism?"

Kylie laughed. Her teeth, but. So perfect. "That's an extreme way to see it, but he wouldn't have drowned."

Too much. I needed wine to process this. On the other hand, I needed to stop turning to wine every time naked women from other planets almost drowned cyclists in revenge for them running over my granddaughter. Out of the blue, Winona spoke. "I need to leave. I'll Translate tonight. Your People are too angry and violent."

I couldn't argue with her—we were. I also wouldn't argue with her because I'd be glad to see the back of her. "Okay." That seemed such a wet response, but that was all I had right then.

She turned that determined stare on Kylie. "You should

complete your task. Your Guardians' reactions are none of my concern, but it will not go well for you if you let them down. You will never become a Guardian yourself if you reveal such a flaw."

Kylie shrugged her off, and I resisted a fist pump. "I will see it done in my own time."

I shouldn't, but what the hell? "Let's open a bottle of wine to see Winona off."

17

Tipsy. Interesting word. Not rat-arsed, but not sober either. Anyway, that was me, tipsy by the time the sun went down, and the darkness wrapped us all in its loving, Winona-removing embrace. She'd said she couldn't Translate—that's definitely the wrong word—inside. They can't enter structures in their natural form, she'd said.

"Bullshit." That must have been the tipsy speaking, I imagine. "Wind and water come into houses all the time."

"Wind and water can enter. We can't. We aren't wind or water. We can control them, but we are the People."

When would it be dark, for god's sake? I couldn't take much more of her self-righteous, self-controlled crap.

At last, darkness came, and we all went out into the back garden. If whispering, "Good riddance," is a tearful goodbye, I gave Winona a tearful goodbye. One second she was there, the next she was gone. My clothes fluttered to the ground in the soft moonlight.

Beside me, Kylie whispered. "She's gone."

"*Thank fu...*" "It must be a sad moment for you."

A few moments of silence. "Not really. I didn't like her. She was too bossy."

"That she was."

We went back inside, and I put *Splash* on the television. Kylie sat beside me now Winona had gone. I couldn't decide whether it was because she no longer felt tied to Winona, she wanted to be close to me, or she just wanted to be able to see the television without getting a stiff neck. I could only decide which one I hoped it had been.

Kylie enjoyed the movie almost as much as Jo had the first time I'd shown it to her. "I see why Grace thought I looked like Madison."

I thought there might be more to the whole mermaid thing than Kylie's slight resemblance to Daryl Hannah, which, let's face it, was restricted to long blonde hair, perfect white teeth, and a figure to die for. When Kylie asked about Daryl, I handed her my iPad, showed her how to use Google, and she read about the actress for quite some time. "I like her." I gave her a quizzical look. "She doesn't eat animals, and she cares about the globe a lot more than most Uprights."

"Yep. She's a regular Greta Thunberg." Off she went to search for the young Swedish woman who'd had such an impact in the environmental arena.

"I like her too. I'd like to meet her."

I laughed. "Just chain yourself to a threatened tree some-where. I'm sure she'll be along eventually."

Kylie studied me for a while, and I grew uncomfortable. "You don't like her?"

"I don't know her, so I couldn't say I don't like her. She's a bit showy for my tastes."

"Your People have had a terrible impact on this globe since we arrived. You don't reside in the Balance. These women are trying to restore some of that, I think."

"Getting rich and famous along the way."

"Abi, this is unlike you. You are a better person than you're pretending to be right now."

I pushed at her, embarrassed and uncertain why I'd tried to act so hard-arsed. Had I been trying to show off? Nah, yeah, nah. Couldn't be that. "It's late, and it's been quite a day. I'm off to bed. Do you want me to drop you at the lake tomorrow?"

She looked down, rubbed her hands together in her lap. At last, she looked up. "Can I stay a few more days? There is more I want to learn. More I want to experience."

My heart leapt. Why I'd asked if she wanted to leave, I couldn't have said, and the second I said it, my heart had turned to ice in my breast. Why her reply made me so happy, I didn't know, but I didn't care either. "Of course."

I lay in bed and closed my eyes, but her smile stayed in my mind. I told myself I enjoyed the company for a change, nothing more. I told myself I'd never found a woman attractive before. I told myself she was no more than a puzzle I wanted to solve. As my hand drifted between my thighs, I told myself I hadn't had sex for ages and I deserved some pleasure after all.

I told myself I'd be quiet.

I lied to myself.

When I woke, I hoped Kylie hadn't heard me last night. That would be the ultimate embarrassment. I would die of shame.

"Good morning." I trilled the greeting as I passed her in the lounge, acting like nothing unusual had happened last night. Did it like a boss.

"Did you have a bad dream?"

I stopped. "No. Why?"

"You screamed sometime in the night."

I died of shame.

18

At some point during the morning, Kylie asked if I had more books she could read. I suggested the library, and by eleven, we were walking into the Belconnen library. I should have taken a photo of her face. She looked like every kid who'd ever been in a candy store, all rolled up into this one, thirty-something woman.

Thirty-something going on millions of years, based on everything they'd told me. It took some understanding. I showed her how the library arranged the books and said I'd pop back when I'd done some shopping. I left her to leaf through as many books as she could while I went over to the mall to buy some groceries, careful to avoid anything that might set her little heart on fire and produce another lecture on the state of the planet.

On the walk over to the mall, I rang Jo to check in on Grace. No lasting effect, it turned out. She had made the most of her accident to wheedle ice cream and extra television time out of her dad. I could tell she was fine.

When I got back to the library, I found Kylie deep in conversation with a young woman with beautiful light brown skin, perhaps of Indian ancestry. They had their heads together and seemed animated, excited by whatever they discussed. They both turned to me as I approached, and I smiled at Kylie. "Ready to head home?"

Instead of Kylie being good to go as I'd expected, she gestured to the woman. "Abi, this is Amisha. She's such a nice person."

Amisha's smile lit up her face as she extended a hand towards me. "Pleased to meet you, Abi."

It amazed me Kylie had managed to latch onto another book addict in the short time I'd been at the mall. Maybe not addict; that sounds awful, but somebody as hooked on reading as Kylie had become. I shook my head, unsure why I felt a little resentment towards Amisha, maybe even jealousy, but my old-fashioned need to be polite took over. "Lovely to meet you too. Amisha, is that right?"

"Call me Mish, please. I've been chatting to Kylie for a while. I teach Information Technology at CIT—"

Kylie interrupted. "That's the Canberra Institute of Technology."

I gave Kylie my most condescending smile. "Yes, Kylie, thanks. I already knew that. I was born here, in case you'd forgotten."

Mish hadn't finished with me. "I noticed Kylie flick through the books, and I was curious, so I asked her about it." I froze my smile in place. We might be about to enter the Twilight Zone again. What had Kylie let slip?

Kylie might have used that sixth sense, or she might have wanted to reassure me she was the soul of discretion and would never reveal her dark secrets to a complete stranger in the library as she read every book in the place in a few hours. Nothing to worry about. "I explained how I like to flick through the books to check whether I'll enjoy them or not."

Not bad, but still so far-fetched I felt sure a technology person wouldn't buy it. Kylie had tried, at least. I had to give her that. I caught my smile before it slipped any further and returned it to its former glory. "Really?"

Mish took over. "It fascinated me, to be honest. Kylie's brain seems to be wired in a unique way." "*If only you knew how unique.*" Mish's brown eyes blazed with enthusiasm and excitement. "It seems she can spot key words, sub-consciously, I suspect, and her brain uses a sort of algorithm to determine whether those words resonate with her. It's remarkable. Unheard of, in fact."

I nodded in a show of solidarity. "She's quite something." I hadn't lied. I'd just left out the part about her being an alien. No need to share everything with Mish. This was our first date, after all. I turned to Kylie again. "Well, we should be going." Back to Mish. "Lovely to have met you." A look at Kylie that brooked no denial, made it clear we didn't need to make any more friends today.

"You too." Amisha's warm smile didn't defrost my icy dread. "I must head off to find some food. I'm so hungry, I could eat the arse out of a low-flying duck."

I joined in with her laughter, then turned to Kylie. "Ready?"

Her face told me she would be happy to stay until she'd read every book in the place, but she swept the look away and replaced it with a smile that brought a flutter to my heart. In the light from that smile, my stern face collapsed on itself, but the grin I returned to Kylie felt like a nervous, frightened thing, afraid to show itself in case the joy hers had given me might escape if I opened my mouth. What was wrong with me? "*Snap out of it, Abi.*"

I bit my tongue as Mish and Kylie hugged, but I smiled with smug satisfaction when they did the bum-out hug that suggested friendship, but not the deep, long-lasting kind where people aren't afraid for their genitals to accidentally touch. We said fond farewells and I marched out. Well, not marched, perhaps. The encounter had been hard on my nerves, and I couldn't quite deny to myself I'd been a tiny bit jealous, with no justification whatsoever. What had this woman done to me?

I asked her how many books she'd read as we walked out to the street, but she didn't know. Lots, it seemed, and she talked about many of them. Some sounded familiar, like "*Animal Farm*," "*Catcher In The Rye*," or "*Big Sur*." Others I didn't recognise at all. I complimented her on the line she'd concocted to throw Amisha off the scent over how fast Kylie read, and she blushed. She looked at me earnestly. "What did she mean about eating the duck?"

I laughed. "It's just an expression. It means she was really hungry. Don't worry. We're not quite that barbaric."

I'd no sooner started the car than Rick rang. I'd been surprised not to hear from him over the weekend. Not disappointed, just surprised. Kylie covered her ears, and I guessed she found my Christopher Cross ringtone loud, or she just didn't like the song. I pushed answer to spare her hearing. Progress. When I was young, if you were out in the car and somebody rang you, you didn't know they'd even called. Now I could answer it from the steering wheel. "Hi Rick."

"Hi Abi. How are you?"

Old fashioned. He'd never dream of opening with some ribald comment about tearing my clothes from my body. Always the same, "How are you?" "I'm okay, thanks."

I hadn't asked him how he was, and the momentary silence suggested he'd noticed. Right now, I didn't really care. I didn't hope he only had days to live or anything, he was just so bloody bland. "What are you doing on Friday night?"

I had no plans, but my mind raced to invent a plausible one. "I have a friend staying with me at the moment." Pathetic, but I've never been good at subterfuge. If I'd been a spy, captured by the Russians, I'd spill the beans within the first five minutes, not because I couldn't tolerate the torture, but because I couldn't think fast enough to make up something false. Okay, I wouldn't have looked forward to the torture either.

"A friend?"

How dull had my life become? His tone suggested he found it implausible I had a friend. That sealed the deal. No date for him on Friday night. "Yes, Rick, a friend. So I can't make any plans, I'm afraid."

I could almost hear his brain whirring as he tried to compute how the call had gone so wrong so fast. "I see. I was going to suggest dinner."

"*Were you?*" I couldn't recall where we were in the on-off situation. A few days ago, I'd been prepared to let him buy me dinner, but now I didn't want a bar of it. I wondered why and cast a quick sideways glance at Kylie. "*Don't be ridiculous, Abi. She'll be gone by Friday, I reckon. Let the man buy you dinner.*"

My brain turned into putty. No, not putty. That has a use. "What about my friend? I can't just leave her alone."

"Bring her with you."

"I can't. She's a vegan." What a pathetic excuse. I'd used her refusal to eat meat like leprosy.

"That's okay. We'll have Indian. There's always a ton of veggie options in an Indian restaurant."

He'd backed me into a corner. "Okay." Where was that vicious lioness from a few days ago? I'd wimped out and couldn't figure out why.

"Great. I'll come round and pick you both up about half six?"

"Sounds good. See you then."

19

He hung up, leaving me disappointed in myself. Rick and I had no future, but instead of cutting the umbilical, I kept letting him back in for another few weeks of frustration, much of it with myself.

Kylie decided to compound my misery. "You're happy for me to stay until Friday?"

Progress. I could answer the phone with my steering wheel, but everybody in the car could hear every word. "I guess so."

"Good. I'm happy to stay."

I risked a quick glance at her. I tried to keep my eyes on the road these days, ever since Mike had been killed. She stared straight ahead, no sign of duplicity in the brief image of her face I took in. "What about your task?"

She didn't reply straight away, but when she did, it surprised me. "Winona has made me wonder about some things, and I want to sort them out in my head before I go to the new water."

"It's not that new, FYI."

"FYI?"

"It means 'for your information.' The lake has been around for a million years. It just ran dry, and now it's got some water in it again."

"I see. I might search the Google about it later. I hadn't realised it was so old."

"Google. Not 'the' Google."

"I see."

I pulled up in the drive and turned the engine off. I grabbed the groceries, put them away, then made us a cup of tea. Kylie sat on the lounge and fiddled with the iPad. I asked if she was hungry, but she wasn't. "What are you looking at?"

She glanced up. "You're right about the water. I can't really grasp the concept of a million of your years, but it's older than I thought."

"This is an ancient country. The first people have been here for over sixty thousand years. White folks only came in the last two or three hundred years."

She looked puzzled. "How can the first Uprights have appeared so recently? I don't know how long ago the Great Catastrophe was, but I'd have thought it was longer ago than that in your years."

I sipped at my tea. Too hot really, but I wanted a distraction while I thought about her question. "Can't answer that, I'm afraid. Maybe you aren't as old as you think you are."

"Maybe." She had returned her attention to the iPad. I watched her type and push and swipe for a while before she spoke again without looking up. "How long can I stay?"

"As long as you like." What the hell? Why had I said that? I scrambled for a recovery position I could retreat to. "As long as Winona doesn't come back."

She laughed, a light, melodic laugh that danced in the air between us, not a Riverdance kind of dance, more of a slow, smoochy dance. I shook my head to dislodge the entwined dancers from my ears. "When can I go to the library again? I like it very much."

"Any time you want, as long as it's open. It's up to you to decide."

"I don't want to put you out though. How far would it be to walk?"

"Far enough. Not too far, but it's quite a walk. I don't mind anyway. I can always drop you and go to see Jo and Grace."

"And Steve."

"Well, yes, but I don't go to see him. I like him, but I go to see Jo and Grace."

"I don't think Jo likes me."

I mean, she wasn't wrong. "Jo doesn't like anyone. Don't worry about it."

"She likes you."

"I'm her mum. She loves me. I don't know whether she likes me."

She tilted her head to one side and pulled out the slight frown. "What is the difference?"

Oh my. How could I explain that? "Don't you know? I thought you had to be like us while you're in that body." Why had I mentioned her body? I wiped my palms on my jeans. Must have been condensation from the teacup, I imagined, the dampness.

"I do, but I don't understand all the emotions Uprights have."

"Uprights doesn't sound very nice, to be honest. Can't you say humans instead?"

The laugh danced out of her mouth again. "I'll try, if it makes you more comfortable."

Comfortable. Not quite the right word for someone whose heart raced like a greyhound on speed, whose palms were sweating, and who had no idea why she had regressed to the thirteen-year-old girl who'd had her first crush on John Bailey, the captain of the under-fifteen rugby team at our school.

Kylie wouldn't let me off the hook. "Explain the difference between like and love, please." She put the iPad on the arm of the lounge, picked up her cup, and cradled it between her hands while she blew on the steaming tea.

I'd have been hopeless on a television quiz show. I knew things, but I often found them difficult to articulate. Let's face it; the difference between like and love is a difficult one. "*I'll take the difference between like and love for five hundred dollars please, Alex.*" I couldn't have answered it for five million dollars, I don't think, but I gave it a stab. "Liking something isn't as intense. When you love something, or somebody, your heart flies around your body when you think about it. Or them. You can't stand to be away from whatever it is you love. It's the first thing you think of in the morning, the last thing you think about at night, and the thing you dream about all night until it's time to wake up and think of it again."

She nodded her head. "I find that difficult to visualise. Other than the heart, are there no physical effects?"

I stalled for time. "Why do you want to know?"

"I'm curious about the difference between the two emotions and how people decide which is which."

I sighed at the rat's nest of explanations required to cover the subject of love. "It's complicated, Kylie. I can say I love pinot noir, and I do. That isn't the same as loving a person, and I don't think I could explain the differences."

"Did you love Mike?"

"I did. We had our problems, but I loved him, and I miss him."

"Have you ever loved a woman?"

Danger, danger. Why had she asked that? "I loved my mum for the first fifteen years or so of my life. I love Jo, and I adore Grace. I love Lucille, but I don't love any of them the way I loved Mike. There's romantic love and love you have for your friends and family. They're different."

She didn't seem to pick up on the comment about my mum, and her laugh sounded less amused, more confused. "It seems complicated."

The breath that exploded from my mouth carried a piece of spit on it. It arced through the air and landed on the coffee table. Embarrassed, I wiped at my lips. "Sorry about that. Yes, it's complicated. Love is a strange beast."

"I'll never understand Upri... humans, perhaps."

"I've been one for forty-nine years, and I don't understand us. I wouldn't expect you to after a week."

"What problems did you and Mike have?"

On the face of it, that had been a rude, highly personal question, but I felt I had to make some allowance for her. She'd only been a human for a week, after all. I didn't feel ready to share everything, even so. I went for a vanilla response. "The usual. Money was tight, especially in the first couple of years of us going alone. We fought about it a lot. Jo was her daddy's girl, and I resented that. He could be a complete dick when he wanted to be, off playing golf when there were things to be done around the house. That's probably true of a lot of marriages, all that stuff. It's tough at times, and you have to get through it one way or another."

"I sense there's more you haven't told me."

I chewed at my lower lip. "Look, this ability you have, or whatever. You can't use it against me like a weapon. You might pick up on my energy or something, whatever it is you do, but you have to learn when to let that pass. Boundaries, that's the word."

"I'm sorry. I have a lot to learn."

She looked so downcast, I reached out and touched the back of her hand. "It's fine. I understand how new all this is to you. It is to me, too. I've never been friends with an alien before. I can't believe I even said that." I felt my cheeks warm up with that uncomfortable burn of embarrassment.

"You would be a good friend. I wish I could stay longer."

Could she hear my heart hammering against my ribs? I hoped not. Why was it doing that, anyway? If I'd answered her earlier question, I'd have said no, I've never loved a woman, and I've never even thought about it before you arrived. I thought back to last night and felt ashamed, humiliated. I'd thought about her while I... I mean, I've paid the single person surcharge before when it came to sex, heaps of times, but I'd never had a woman's face in my head before. I needed to escape this situation and my own feelings. "What do you want for dinner?"

"Aloo gobi." She answered without a thought.

"Aren't you bored of it?"

"We haven't had it for days."

I gave in. She had an innocent's joy about all the things she liked, and I didn't want to crush it out of her. The world would do that for me, if she hung around long enough, as I knew from bitter experience. I liked her naïve views on everything, how simply she saw things. She was right. We had buggered the world up, and we could use a reset where we all saw things with the simple gaze of a child and learned to value what we had again.

Shit. Would she turn me into a vegan? I hoped not.

20

On Wednesday, I went to Jo's place and spent a couple of hours with them after I'd dropped Kylie at the library. I'd tried to have a conversation with Kylie about how she might come across some authors whose views would be very different from hers, or who had revealed some ugly side to their personalities in their non-author lives, but nothing could quash her burning desire to consume the written word. She was a sponge. If not for the library, she would have bankrupted me within a fortnight if I had to buy books for her. To describe her appetite for books as voracious would flatter the most voracious thing on Earth.

As I had dreaded, Jo quizzed me endlessly about Kylie. When was she leaving? Whereabouts at Lake George did she live? Why had I put her up in my house for so long? What had been Winona's real name, because Jo couldn't accept it could be Winona? I ducked and dodged, weaved and swerved like a champion boxer as I held her relentless onslaught at bay.

Grace showed no sign of trauma from the accident and

proudly showed me her plasters as though she was showing off all the major trophies from some sport or other. She was a tough little cookie, like her mum. Not her grandmother so much, these days.

Jo made no secret of her distrust of Kylie, and I argued on the stranger's behalf as much as I could, told Jo she was a good person who was easy company in the evenings when the doldrums would normally come a-calling. I tried not to go over-board on the praise. I was confused enough about how I felt about her without Jo chiming in if she suspected I might have even the slightest attraction to Kylie. The truth was, I couldn't deny it to myself anymore. For whatever reason, I did feel something.

I couldn't describe it, I couldn't have explained it. It wasn't as simple as finding her attractive. Stevie Wonder could see how gorgeous she was. It wasn't lust. I felt drawn to her some-how. It might have been the strange mystique of a dream of a relationship with an alien. It sounded exotic when I put it that way.

I reminded myself Stevie Wonder jokes were in poor taste and felt an appropriate amount of guilt, but the entire time, I longed to head over to the library and collect Kylie, to bask in that bizarre personality, to look into those pure, guileless green eyes, to see that amazing figure, that great arse... Oops.

Grace asked about her, too. To be fair, she asked about the mermaid, but I presumed she meant Kylie and not that little sourpuss Winona. Grace was in fine form, insisting I help her with her colouring book, her favourite thing, for this week at least, Jo said.

To my surprise, when I went back to the library, Kylie wanted to walk around the lake for a time, so we set off. She had some choice words for whoever had approved the new concrete apartment building across the road from the lake, where the old mall car park had once been. Some of the units looked lived-in now. It had taken a long time to build through the COVID pandemic. That had been a hellish time, and I hoped we'd never see its like again.

The units must have awesome views over the lake, but I agreed the building itself didn't offer the lake a similar bargain, all concrete and glass. We walked along the western edge of the lake, and a choir of sulphur-crested cockatoos swooped and soared overhead as they screeched their raucous hymn to the day, so loud, they made conversation impossible. Kylie covered her ears, and I muttered under my breath at the noise. "Bloody cockies." There could surely be no noisier bird anywhere on earth, but Kylie watched them in awe, her eyes wide, her hands over her ears.

They passed out of earshot, and I explained how destructive they could be. They dug holes everywhere in any piece of lawn they took a fancy to, and they could destroy the woodwork on a house or a balcony in no time flat. She pointed out they were part of the Balance. I kept my thoughts on that bit of the Balance to myself. She wouldn't have appreciated them.

We reached Yerra beach, where she had first appeared, and she stood on the sand as she gazed out across the lake towards the peninsula in the middle. I sat on the same bench I'd been on that day, only a week ago. I spotted my coffee cup, abandoned in the sand, and I stood to pick it up. Kylie turned, and she had a tear in her eye. I reached for her. "What's wrong?"

"I don't know. The water just came out of my eyes when I thought about the day I left my life in this water behind."

Miserable, I made a suggestion I knew I'd live to regret if she followed it. "You could go back in."

A sad smile came to her lips, and it drew me into her unhappiness. "Of all the things I could do, that is the one thing I cannot."

"*Well, thank fu...*" "Come on, let's head back. This place makes you sad." It didn't make me sad, because I'd first met her here, but I didn't say that. It sounded pathetic, soppy even.

That night, I took myself off to bed early, but not because I was tired. I'd decided only one person could help me with these feelings. Lucille. I needed her now as much as she'd ever needed me. "Hi sweetie." Her voice made me feel better the second I heard it.

We exchanged some small talk, then I decided to cut to the chase. "I need your help. Advice, really, more than help."

"Ask it, babe. I'd do anything for you, you know that."

"I can't really talk about it on the phone. Can we catch up for coffee as soon as poss?"

"I feel a bug coming on. I can call in sick tomorrow."

What a friend. Friends like Lucille don't come along that often, and I considered myself lucky to have found mine. "That's great. Usual place, around twelve?"

"Sounds good. What about your friends?"

"Friend, singular. One of them has moved on. I'll drop the other one at the library in Civic. She'll love it. I'll explain it all tomorrow. Love you."

"Love you more." Lucille's usual farewell. I thought it was a bit cringe, but it was her, and I loved her.

I hadn't lied. Kylie would adore the library in the city centre. It was way bigger than Belconnen library, and she'd find books there she might not often see in Belco. It might even be difficult to get her to leave, I reckoned.

21

I told her about the library at breakfast, and she became so excited, I hoped it wouldn't let me down and disappoint her. She felt miserable when I said I'd meet Lucille while she read, keen to come, but I couldn't allow that, so I laid it on thick, told her she shouldn't blame herself, that reading was her jam, a word I'd picked up from one of Mike's Rage Against The Machine albums. I assured her Lucille would understand.

We got to the Canberra Centre early because I wanted to walk down to the library with her rather than risk her getting lost. I didn't want her to get into a scrape and have to dive into Lake Burley Griffin to escape a horde of pitchfork-wielding locals. What if she couldn't come out once she'd gone in? I might never see her again. I told myself to grow up and left her at the door with strict instructions not to leave until I came back for her.

I wandered back to the café. I arrived bang on time, which made me ten minutes early. Impatient, I waited for Lucille. I checked all the staff to see whether that same dweeb of a waiter had been rostered on, but I didn't see him. Lucille was five minutes later than usual, but she breezed in like always, content to be herself and screw what anybody else thought. She wore a bright, striped pair of trousers I wouldn't have been seen dead in, but that was Lucille. She answered to herself and nobody else.

We ordered coffee and a toastie each, and she placed a hand over mine. "What's eating you, babe?"

I took a deep breath and promptly forgot the speech I'd rehearsed for most of the sleepless night. "I'm worried about Kylie."

"So, Kylie's the one who left?"

Bugger. I'd messed the whole thing up from the start. "No. She's the one who stayed. The problem is her. Well, no, it's me. I think I..." I glanced around to check nobody was eavesdropping, dropped my voice to a whisper. "I think I fancy her."

Lucille hadn't got the memo about the surreptitious part of the conversation. She leaned back and almost shouted, and I scrunched myself up as small as I could so nobody would notice me. "Well, look at you. A bit late in your life to realise you're queer, isn't it?"

I beseeched her to spare me some dignity. "Shh. I'm not queer, and I'm not even sure we're allowed to say that. I just feel something whenever I'm with her. And when I'm not. Damn it."

"First of all, I'm trans, darling, and I'm allowed to say queer as much as I want. And so are you, now you've got the hots for Miss Perfect."

Still too loud, Lucille. "Shh. I haven't got the hots for her.

Christ, I thought you were going to help me, not embarrass me so much I can never show my face in the city again."

"I can't say I blame you, Abi. I mean, she is hot af."

I grimaced. "Yeah, I don't even know what that means."

"That hair, those teeth, that body. Ooh la la."

I tried to make myself even smaller, and the waiter brought our coffees. I flashed a thank-you smile. "Lucille, focus. It's not like that. I just feel something for her, and it's more than friendship. The other night I pictured her while I... you know."

"Oh my god. You have her in your wank bank?"

"That's disgusting. Truly gross. What should I do?"

"Take her home and fuck her."

I looked around, mortified. Nobody stared at us, but they stared at their food and drinks. I knew they were listening and loving my total humiliation. "I can't just do that. What if she doesn't want to? She's half my age, for god's sake."

"She is not half your age. How old is she?"

"Thirty-one."

I didn't care for the low, appreciative whistle she loosed. "She looks good for that age. I'd have said twenty-five. So would that waiter on Saturday. He had the hots for her in a big way."

My words surfed out of my mouth on waves of derisory laughter. "Yes, well, the feeling wasn't mutual, I can assure you."

"You're, what, forty-eight?"

"Forty-nine."

"Eighteen years. That's nothing. Go for it."

I threw my head back in despair and almost skittered the toasties out of the waiter's hands. Several profuse apologies later, I returned to the conversation. "You aren't helping. How can I be gay now, at forty-nine? I've never fancied a woman; I've never kissed one. I've only ever been with Mike."

"Abi dear, I told you when that bastard betrayed you—"

I couldn't sit by and let her impugn Mike's honour like that. "His name's Mike, and he didn't betray me, he had a momentary lapse in judgement."

"He shagged someone else for over a year. He betrayed you." Her face suggested any argument on the matter would be futile and even, perhaps, harmful to my health. "I told you to leave him then. You deserved so much more than that boring bean-counter."

I don't know why I persisted with my urgent whispers. Maybe in the hope Lucille would lower her own voice at some point in harmony with me. I jabbed a finger into my chest for emphasis. "I'm a boring bean-counter."

"Not so boring now though, are you? You've got a hottie, you've got a hottie."

If anything, she was getting louder, and the sing-song chant at the end of her last answer could probably have been heard in Civic library. Kylie had probably already dived into Lake BG so she'd never have to face me again. "Will you please lower your voice? I haven't got her at all. For all I know, she'd be horrified if she knew. She thinks I'm her friend, but here I am letting her down by confessing to you that I'd like to... You know."

"You need to go for it, I reckon. What's the worst that could happen? She slaps your face."

Lucille, of course, didn't know the consequences could be so much worse. Kylie could blow me up in the air and drop me, arse first, onto the spire at the top of the Telstra tower. So much worse than a slap to the face. I squirmed, a little uncomfortable at the mere thought. "You're no help at all. I might as well have taken out a full-page ad in the Times and asked for the public's opinions."

"Look, Abi. If you like her, tell her. It's the best way. Unrequited love will drive you nuts, I promise you. It's like a yeast infection you can't clear up."

"Well, that's gross. Thanks for that."

"You have to take the plunge and tell her, babe. Be honest with her and see what she says."

"What if she says no?"

Lucille studied me for a moment while I took a mouthful of my toastie. "If she says no, she's crazy. You're scared she's too good for you because she looks so smoking hot, but it's the other way around. She needs to check herself if she doesn't realise you're the best thing that could happen to her, even if it didn't last long."

It would be a short fling, if it happened at all, but I couldn't tell Lucille that. "Well, thanks for saying that, even if it is a crock. What about Jo?"

Lucille almost spat her piece of toastie out. "What about Jo? You carried her in your womb for nine months, you fed her, you clothed her until she could move out and stand on her own two feet. You don't owe her a thing."

"She mightn't like it, her mum turning gay at forty-nine."

"It's none of her bloody business though, is it? Screw her. Do it."

"There's Grace to think about."

"Grace is a kid. Modern kids get all this stuff. She'll grow up proud of her queer nana." Lucille's laugh could call the cows home, and I urged her again to keep it down a bit.

"I feel like I'd be betraying Mike."

"You should have left him. I told you at the time."

I sighed. "I don't know what to do. I don't know anything about being with another woman."

"That's easily solved. When you pick her up from the library, borrow the book, '*How To Be A Lesbian.*'"

"There's a book about it?"

She smacked the top of my arm. It hurt, and I rubbed it. "Of course there isn't a book about it, you numpty. You know exactly what to do with her. All the things that bastard never did with you. Touch all the things he couldn't find. That's bound to work."

"Mike." I felt I had to remind her of his name. "And he was good in bed."

"Well, we know that, don't we? Half the women in Canberra know that, because he probably shagged them all."

"I'm picking up a bit of hostility here, as though you resent him in some way."

"You think?"

"Thank you for your loyalty, but can we focus on Kylie please? How can I have any feelings for her? Why has this happened now, after all these years?"

She drew an hourglass in the air and rolled her eyeballs up into her lids. "When someone comes gift-wrapped like that, honey, you don't ask why."

"That's sexist. You're a misogynistic disgrace to humanity."

"I may be, but you're over-thinking this. You're attracted to someone. So she happens to be a woman. We wouldn't be having this conversation if you felt this way about Rick."

I snorted. "We wouldn't. I'd be locked away, for my own good. He's so boring."

"Go. For. It. Talk to her. Tonight. The longer you leave it, the more chance you'll accidentally let it slip anyway."

"You have to tell Jo. I can't do that."

She roared with laughter. "You're scared of your own daughter."

"She's vicious. You don't know her like I do. She nearly killed some guy at the weekend when he ran Grace over with his bike."

The teasing stopped, and worry swamped her face. "Is she okay? I might have killed him for that."

"She's fine." Jo hadn't been the one who almost killed him, either, but I felt plenty of trepidation about telling Lucille the truth about who had. "She ran in front of him, just an accident."

"You can't be afraid of your own daughter. Again, what's the worst that can happen? Jo disowns you and refuses to let you leave everything to her in your will?" I couldn't find a suitable retort. "Grace will love it. A gay grannie. She'll be proud of you."

"She's three, for fu... She doesn't know anything about gays."

"I wouldn't be too sure of that. Kids today are a lot more mature than we were."

"This toastie is more mature than you."

Her ironic smile did nothing for my iron levels. "Thank you. I love you too."

Lucille was right, I supposed. I did feel some attraction to Kylie, and if I told her, I'd have nothing to lose. She intended to leave anyway, so what difference if she wanted to go out to the lake a day or two early? "Okay, I'll tell her."

"Call me straight after, no pun intended. I have to know what happens."

"I hate you." I didn't mean it.

22

I didn't quite have to threaten Kylie with the cops to get her out of the library, but they were mentioned. She insisted on a few more books, and even though I felt stupid, I took the chance to check the library didn't have a copy of *"How To Be A Lesbian"* or something similar, then realised what a complete idiot I'd been and dragged her out of the library and to the car.

I didn't tell her how I felt that night, although we drank a bottle of wine between us as I tried to summon up the courage. It had sounded so easy when Lucille had told me to do it in the café, but my nerves frayed, I shook like a leaf, and I couldn't drag the words out of my throat and give them voice. Lucille called around nine thirty, and a cryptic conversation took place so Kylie couldn't guess we were talking about her. Lucille called me several names and used her colourful language to its fullest extent. I couldn't argue with her; she was right. I had chickened out, and when I hung up, I gave Kylie a nervous smile. She didn't look at all nervous, and I envied her on so many levels, not least her flawless good looks and OMFG body. I felt guilty when I thought back to that body, dripping and naked at the lake. Had I objectified her? Could I even do it with her, given her vulnerable other-worldly nature?

I went to bed before I said or did something I'd regret, then lay awake for an hour filled with regret because I hadn't said or done anything.

Thursday. The day I once again didn't say anything. We walked down to the local café for a coffee. I'd been there many times in recent years and was on first name terms with the owner, Leslie.

Leslie smiled at me. "Good morning, Abi."

I planned to order a decaf espresso for Kylie, still unsure how her non-human body would react to such a renowned stimulant. I batted away Leslie's concerns as my face flushed and sweat droplets formed on my forehead, just like every time I thought words like, "body," or, "stimulant." I felt twelve again, and not in a good way.

As I drew in a breath to order, I glanced at the blackboard with the bewildering array of potential coffees available to those with varying tastes. I noticed the words, "Soy milk," and after I checked with Leslie that it was vegan, I ordered Kylie a decaf, soy milk flat white. Kylie seemed delighted to have a coffee that resembled my own, and after the first sip, she said she loved it as I wiped the foam moustache from her upper lip.

When Lucille rang, I answered, said, "No," and hung up on her. I couldn't take her disdain. I had enough of my own without a pile-on from her.

Friday. At last. Rick's car pulled up in the drive and I could forget the abject misery of another day of unrequited feelings for a couple of hours. I did try to raise the subject, but every time, the alternatives, such as being turned into a pillar of salt, seemed more attractive.

I'd loaned Kylie some clothes again, and they didn't fit again, but she still somehow looked spectacular again, and I died a little more inside again. I pulled the door open and gave a little gasp of surprise as Rick kissed me on the cheek. Perhaps he'd been to the library for a copy of "*How To Date A Woman*."

I waved towards Kylie. "Rick, this is my friend, Kylie. Kylie —Rick."

I'd briefed her on the Perth story and the vague, on-off relationship. I'd been nervous to say much about him in case it somehow turned her off me, as if she'd given me one single buying signal since she arrived. Still, better safe than sorry. "Nice to meet you, Rick. I've heard so much about you."

Where had she learned that line? She'd heard next to nothing about him, and none of it good. I looked down at my shoes, wiped an imaginary spot of dirt from the carpet with the sole of one. I felt guilty about going to dinner with Rick when I had no interest in him, but I'd been glad of the the chance to get out and not be trapped alone in the house with this Mata Hari who sat, so near and yet so far, on the lounge with me, teased me with her smile as well as her pout, and laughed at my favourite movies, jokes, and stories.

Rick drove us down to the lake and we sat at a table in the Indian restaurant. His eyebrows shot up when I ordered a bottle of wine, but the day had been hell, and I needed the alcohol to relax me. Kylie had been a nightmare, like a siren leading me towards temptation with hideous acts of treachery such as breathing, laughing, speaking, going to the bathroom— I'd tried all day not to stare at her bum, but with little success. She had even coughed once, but hadn't had the good grace to follow up on it by collapsing to the floor, close to death and affording me the chance to administer mouth-to-mouth resuscitation. Evil witch much?

Rick couldn't tell a joke to save his life, so let's hope he never enters a, "Crack the audience up or die," competition. That had never stopped him from trying, sadly, and tonight he was in the best form of his life. "What's the difference between a buffalo and a bison?"

Kylie frowned as she seemed to search that encyclopaedic mind. "Bison are indigenous to North America, while buffalo can be found on other continents. Also, bison have a beard and a humped shoulder, while—"

He interrupted, a little crestfallen, I thought. "No, it's that you can't wash your hands in a bison."

I gave Kylie a second to laugh. She didn't. "I think it's the other way round, Rick. You can't wash your hands in a buffalo." Kylie still didn't laugh. I should have warned her about his jokes.

Unabashed, he laughed. "Silly me."

"*Yep. Silly you, you dry old goat.*"

I groaned as he took a mouthful of massaman, then launched into another attempt to humiliate himself. "The brown paper cowboy rides into town in his brown paper shirt, brown paper trousers, and brown paper boots." This had all the hallmarks of a long one. Those were even worse when you knew the denouement would be massacred by the world's least funny man. "Sheriff says, 'Are you the brown paper cowboy?' The brown paper cowboy says, 'Sheriff, I'm wearing my brown paper shirt, brown paper trousers, and brown paper boots. I am that brown paper cowboy.'" I'd been right. Long, tedious, and ultimately disappointing. "The sheriff says, 'Son, I'm arresting you.' The brown paper cowboy looks stunned and asks why, so the sheriff says, 'Stealing cows.'"

I frowned. The failed joke made no sense. Kylie reached over and laid a hand on his, to my surprise and jealousy. "I think you meant 'rustling.'" She laughed. "It's funny, because it's a play on words."

He joined her laughter, and I wondered if I could slip something into his massaman. Kylie wouldn't eat it, and I could avoid it too, play the empathy card with Kylie as he choked to death like Joffrey in Game Of Thrones. He confessed to his total lack of ability. "I'm hopeless at jokes. You're right. Rustling."

In a different time and place, I would have laughed at the joke, if I'd heard it from someone who told it properly instead of the mangled word salad this buffoon had just spewed. How had Kylie worked it out? Their jovial laughter proved too much for me to bear, so I ordered a second bottle of wine. To add insult to injury, she launched into a joke I'd told her. I clenched my fists under the table. Why did she want to entertain this jackass instead of falling into bed with me? "Two southsiders walk into a bar. You'd think one of them would have noticed it."

He roared with laughter at *my* joke. Not mine as in I'd made it up, but I'd told it to her. But for me, she wouldn't have known the joke in the first place. I skulled the last of the wine in my glass.

That's when I wrecked everything.

23

I turned to Kylie, leaned in closer. "You're funny." I don't doubt I'd slurred the words, but I didn't slur the next bit. I pressed my face close to hers and kissed her on the lips. Not a long kiss. I didn't slobber over her or force my tongue between her teeth. I didn't drag her onto the table and ravish her right there in the basmati rice and the spilt red lentil curry from when I'd tried for an empathy badge. Just a peck on the lips, nothing more. I pulled my head back, slow, horrified.

What had I done? In the space of a few seconds, I had become a sexual predator. I had touched her—kissed her— without permission. Disgraceful. I'd be locked up, and they'd throw the key away. I imagined the court scene as the paparazzi snapped photos of my shame for the Canberra Times.

"How do you plead, Mrs Lucas?"

"I'm guilty, but society's to blame. I acted out of unrequited lust and uncontrolled drunkenness. I throw myself on the mercy of the court."

Gavel slams down onto the block. "Life imprisonment with no chance of parole."

Tears trickled from my eyes in my imagination and in real life. I breathed the only inadequate, horrified thing I could think of. "I'm sorry."

I sat upright in my chair. The silence at the table deafened me. You could have sliced Rick's outrage up with a blunt knife and slapped it onto the barbecue. His judgement burned into me like a red-hot poker. Kylie looked at me with her head on one side, but she said nothing. Her emotionless eyes gave nothing away, but she didn't drag me onto the table and ravish me, so I presumed the kiss hadn't landed on fertile ground.

Rick broke the silence. "What's that about, Abi?"

Even in the depths of my embarrassment, I realised I didn't owe Rick any explanation of what lay behind the moment. "That's between Kylie and me."

He swivelled his eyes to Kylie. The accusation faded in that one second, replaced by sympathy, understanding, and shared indignation. "Are you okay, love?" I ground my teeth. His righteous indignation at my treatment of Kylie meant nothing when he took it upon himself to use condescending, demeaning phrases like, "Love," to a woman he barely knew. Arsehole

Kylie nodded. "Yes, I'm fine. No harm done. Just a friendly kiss." She smiled a smile that would have melted me, but imagine my disappointment when Rick didn't dissolve into a pile of slime and trickle from the chair onto the floor and out of my life.

He huffed. Or harrumphed. Rick was more of a harrumpher, I think, on reflection. "Well, it didn't look that way to me."

Kylie's smile didn't change in the least. "I don't think it's your place to decide, Rick."

His face. I almost picked up my phone to take a picture. All right, I did try to pick up my phone for a picture, but drunken fingers refused my commands and knocked it to the floor. If I didn't love her before... Well, I still didn't love her, but I respected the hell out of her for that answer. I was more than a little relieved as well. At least she hadn't stormed off.

The atmosphere at the table turned frigid. Rick's empathy disappeared in the last fading echo of Kylie's words. I'd never seen him look the way he did at that moment, and I couldn't decide what he might do. I decided to call the proceedings to a halt. "I think it's time to head home, don't you? I'll pay the bill."

He stared at me, a vehemence behind his eyes I wouldn't have thought him capable of. I patted my head to make sure my hair hadn't caught fire under the ferocity of his glare. I was drunker than I realised. I stood, retrieved my phone without falling flat on my face, and slithered over to the counter. I paid the bill, and when I turned, he had gone.

Rick had vanished. Not like Winona had vanished. He hadn't left his clothes behind. I almost threw up at the thought of him naked. Where had he gone? I suppose he must have left while I battled the uneven ground between my chair and the counter. It must have been uneven. Why else had I taken such a circuitous route, grateful for the occasional chair I could grip the back of? What an arsehole. He'd abandoned us, thrown us out like a worn-out sock. At least he hadn't taken Kylie and left me alone. That would have been the last straw.

I gave Kylie a half-hearted smile. "Looks like we need an Uber."

She nodded, accompanied by a small laugh. "It does."

"What did he say?"

"Nothing. He just stood up and left."

"Prick."

Kylie stood. "Let's get home. It feels like you might have something you want to tell me."

Had she worked that out herself, or had she known all along thanks to that inexplicable sixth sense thing she said she had? It felt uncomfortable to think she might know everything I ever thought or felt, but what could I do about it? Take her out to Lake George or live with it. I resigned myself to living with it.

As luck would have it, we got one of those quiet Uber drivers, not one of the chatty, irrepressibly cheerful ones. I had no chat or cheer available to bandy small talk with a stranger who didn't realise a predator sat in their back seat.

A few minutes and a couple of mumbled thanks later, his headlights disappeared up the street, and I dropped the front door key. Kylie laughed, bent, and picked the keys up. She opened the door, turned on the light, and went straight to the lounge. I stood nearby, uncertain, unsteady, and she patted the cushion next to herself. "Sit before you fall down."

I accepted the invitation. "I'm sorry, Kylie. I don't know what came over me. It was inappropriate, and I understand your anger."

"I'm not angry. You're attracted to me, you had too much wine, and if you didn't try to become intimate with me, you would have only had Rick available. He has the personality of a piece of blank paper, so you decided to seduce me."

My mouth was open, but it closed by itself as I made a sort of snarl-like grunt that passed for an amazed laugh. How had she come up with that pile of BS? It would have been laughable if it hadn't been almost true. "Those aren't the words I would have used."

"You speak English better than me. I am too formal at times. I'm trying to improve."

I didn't give a rat's arse about her English. "I shouldn't have kissed you without permission."

"How do you know I didn't permit it?"

I snorted again. "Because I didn't ask, which I should have done."

She sat there, lost in some thought, and I waited for her to say something else. I did a pretty good job of not kissing her again and felt proud of myself, but I imagined it, a proper kiss, tongues and everything. When she sucked in a long breath, I knew the rejection was about to arrive, along with a request for a lift to Lake George in the morning. I choked on my misery and gave a cough. My heart felt so heavy, I hoped the muscles around it could support the weight or it might drop down into my stomach. Did muscles hold it in place? The heart is a muscle, so maybe it held itself in place, but—

Thank goodness she interrupted the futile chain of thought. "The Guardians warned me not to mate with an Upright. They claimed I might divide, and they feared what form that division might take if I mated with one of your kind."

I squinted at her as I tried to unravel it all. "I beg your pardon? What is 'divide?'"

"You would say pregnant, I believe. If I mate with you, I might get pregnant."

I tried not to laugh. It would be rude to laugh, but I couldn't help myself. "I might get you pregnant? That's ridiculous. Two women can't get each other pregnant. You'd have needed to do it with Rick for that, and even then..." Uncharitable, and speculation. He might be fertile enough to populate a small country for all I knew, and he might be dynamite in bed, a real Casanova.

"That's what I thought, but the Guardians were quite clear."

I waved a hand about in a dismissive gesture. "Screw the Guardians. You wouldn't get pregnant. Neither would I."

"We could mate in safety?"

I shook my head, bewildered by the weird way she spoke at times. "Don't use that phrase. It sounds bloody awful. We wouldn't be mating, we'd be making love, or having sex. Or shagging."

"I see." She glanced down at her lap. "Would you like to be doing the shagging with me?"

I laughed at her clumsy attempt to use a more appropriate term. "Of course I'd like to have sex with you. You're perfect. Who wouldn't want to?" Lucille would be stoked. I'd done it. I'd admitted I fancied her. In fact, I'd gone further, straight into new territory, accepting that I wanted to do the deed with her. I'd changed teams. Goodbye Rick with your lousy jokes and your five-series Beemer, hello Kylie with your alien history and your ability to read a book in three seconds. Could I satisfy her? Too late for that now. I'd taken the leap, and only time would tell whether I could take her to the dizzy heights of satisfaction for which she must yearn.

"I'm not perfect—"

"Look in a mirror, honey. You're a ten. No. You go up to eleven."

Note to self: play *Spinal Tap* for Kylie. She ignored my compliment. "Perfection is a construct based on the existence of competition." What? This wasn't the pillow talk I'd hoped for. "That is the problem with your kind. You deify everything. You strive to achieve the best outcome, the best result, when you should accept there are no measures of better or worse. You worship the best, you strive to be the best, and you vilify anything less than the best. I'm not perfect, because for me to be perfect requires someone else to be imperfect. In that situation, you will deify me for my good looks and vilify another for their lack of them. That is not the way to reside in the Balance."

I stared at her, dumbstruck as I resisted the old joke, the one where I ask her if she'd swallowed a dictionary. If ever that joke would miss the mark, it would be with Kylie. A few seconds ago, I'd felt she was almost ready to leap into bed with me. Now I felt like a first-year philosophy student with the strictest, harshest professor in the history of strict, harsh professors. I spluttered a feeble attempt at a response. "I don't reside in your Balance. We aren't like you."

She nodded as an expression of miserable disappointment spread across her face. "I know. That is how you have become. At one time, you were like us, and you resided in the Balance."

"I'm sorry Kylie, I want more from my existence than some intangible joy because I've lived my boring life to the best interest of something I can't see, touch, or understand. I want to live, to feel the wind in my hair, the sun on my face, the joys of someone else's body. Somebody else's hands on my body." I might have gone a bit far, perhaps, but I couldn't see any prospect of me finding her Balance or the human race becoming whatever she believed we used to be.

Her face told me the answer had hurt, and guilt washed over me. At the same time, as much as I wanted her, and at that moment, my desire for her physically hurt, I could see no way to change the fact that I was human, and she wasn't. If that meant we wanted different things, I couldn't fix it, and as frustrating as that would be for me, it would be best if I didn't go on driving myself crazy with lust for her. "I'm sorry. I'll take you home tomorrow." A tear fell from my eye, landed on my trousers. "I'm going to bed. I've buggered everything up and hurt you in the process. Not one of my proudest moments. Good night, Kylie."

"Good night, Abi." She managed a weak smile, this amazing creature who had come out of the lake bent on one purpose, but who had brought a light into my life for a few days that now looked as though it would be snuffed out. I'd return to my humdrum routine, just another disappointment to chalk up on the blackboard of a life that had never quite made the grade. Whenever it came close, something stepped in to screw it all up; Mike, Jo, the woman Mike had the affair with, the drunk driver...

I wouldn't add Kylie to that list. She was different, even though the outcome would be the same. I'd go on. I'd get over my silly, schoolgirlish infatuation. I'd spend time with Jo and Grace. I might find another Rick, maybe even somebody I actually liked.

I cried myself to sleep.

24

I felt terrible in the morning. I had a stink hangover: dry mouth, pounding head, sore eyes, bilious stomach. More than that, I'd made such a mess of the situation with Kylie, I doubted it could be recovered even if she wanted it to be.

I could tell myself I'd never drink again, but I'd tried that before. Mired in the depths of a hangover, drinker's remorse could be strong enough to permit the prospect of never touching a drop again. It never lasted; empty, pointless promises that would be broken the next time things got tough.

I didn't know whether I should drive right away or wait for some blood to find its way into the pure alcohol that must have been running through my veins. I lay there for a while and studied my ceiling as I wondered what I could have done better. To have stayed sober would have been a good start. Perhaps not have involved Rick in the Greek tragedy I turned the night into. If I'd had the courage to take Lucille's advice earlier, none of this might have happened.

I forced myself into the shower, dressed, then went into the lounge. Kylie glanced up from the iPad as I appeared. Her warm smile lit up the room. "Good morning, Abi. How do you feel today?"

"Like death warmed up."

She pulled her usual thinking-about-that face. "Then you must feel terrible."

"I do. Look, about last night. I'm sorry—"

"Please don't apologise again." She'd interrupted me, but I didn't feel anger or resentment. "You didn't do anything to apologise for."

"Rick wouldn't agree with you."

"He doesn't matter. He isn't my friend. What he is to you is none of my business. You're my friend, and I'm asking you to forgive yourself."

I perched on the edge of one of the dining chairs. "Can you forgive me?"

"I have nothing to forgive you for. I've already told you that. You did nothing wrong. You kissed me, that's all." She made it sound like a peck on the cheek from a moderately okay auntie, not the expression of all the desire I'd built up inside myself over the week leading up to it. "I liked it."

I guffawed. "Yeah, me too." I'd reached the kitchen before I registered what she'd said. She'd liked it? "You liked it?"

"I did." She nodded, a sharp confirmation of her words.

Why hadn't she said that last night instead of banging on about perfection and the stupid Balance? I filled the jug, flicked the switch. I pulled mugs out of the cupboard, poured milk into both of them, tipped it out of one of them and rinsed it, all absent-minded as I pondered what the implications might have been, still could be, perhaps.

I put the mugs of tea on the coffee table I never put coffee on and dropped onto the lounge next to her. "Why didn't you say that last night?" I wished I'd had some better line, but none had come to me.

"Would it have made any difference?"

I didn't know, now she'd asked the question. It might have made me feel better about the faux pas in the restaurant. I realised I'd made it all about me, when it should be about her. She'd enjoyed the kiss, but that didn't excuse the way I'd kissed her. "I still should have made sure you were comfortable with it before I did it."

"You were impetuous. I like that about you. You act without thinking."

"Fat lot of good that's done me so far." Again with the, "just thinking that, ended up saying it."

Kylie sipped at her tea. "What shall we do today?"

My heart pounded like the drums in that Todd Rundgren song about pounding on drums. She hadn't asked when I would take her out to Lake George, but for the sake of my last remaining nerve, I decided to check. "Don't you want to go out to Lake George?"

"I don't. There are more books in the library I want to read." I stared at her, staggered, then the twitch at the corners of her mouth told me I'd been played. I slapped at the top of her arm. "I want to go somewhere outside Canberra if that's possible. I'd like to see more of the countryside. Not to the water though."

It sounded as though she'd added the last sentence as an afterthought, reassurance for me more than anything else. "Okay, we'll head out to Hall or somewhere. After I eat some breakfast first. I don't want to drive until I soak up some of that booze from last night."

I scrambled some eggs for me, spread some avocado on toast for Kylie. As we chewed our way through it, which took a while for me as I battled the weariness and the urge to throw up, I had a thought. "We could go to the mall on the way back if you like. We could buy you some clothes of your own. You must be sick of mine."

The slow, rhythmical nod suggested she saw some reason not to agree with my suggestion. "What will you do with them afterwards?"

She'd raised the implication of the eventual trip to the lake, something I hadn't considered. I didn't want to think about that, so I focused on my eggs. "Give them away. Go on a diet until I can wear them. Who knows? Who cares?"

Her laughter rekindled the dimmed light deep in my core. "Okay, let's do it. See? I can be impetuous too."

I turned my head. Her eyes sparkled, and so did her teeth, come to think of it. So white. The little creases at the edge of her mouth from her massive grin weren't quite dimples, but damn, they looked great. Her long hair hung around shoulders that shook with the gentle laughter. She looked incredible, and I gulped. I wasn't proud of my reaction, but my heart had turned to goo, and she was making daggers with it, then stabbing me in the naughty bits with them.

She leaned forward and kissed me, a gentle, tender brush of four lips together, then she pulled back and smiled a soft smile that finished me off. I almost fainted, and I dropped my knife and fork so I could hold the edge of the table. My breath must reek after last night, and I wondered whether she would say anything about it, but she said nothing.

Christopher Cross couldn't have chosen a worse time to sing at me from the kitchen bench. I considered ignoring it but thought of Grace. I couldn't live with myself if something had happened and I'd ignored the phone for an avocado-flavoured kiss. The chair scraped against the wooden floor like the fingernails that scratched across my heart as I broke the spell of that magical moment.

Rick? For fu... "What?"

"How are you and your lady friend this morning?"

"Why do you care?"

"I felt guilty that I left you behind, so I went back. They said you'd called an Uber. I wanted to apologise for that. It wasn't very gentlemanly."

Was "gentlemanly" even a word? "It's fine. We made it home safe and sound. Thanks for your concern."

"I want you to know I'm still not happy about you and her. I hoped you and I could make a go of it, but if you're going to be unfaithful..."

I twisted my mouth as I tried for a suitable response. "Go to hell, Rick." I hung up. Not my best work, but it had been concise and unambiguous, so there was that.

I finished the eggs, we put the dishes in the dishwasher, and we went off to clean our teeth. I felt that same schoolgirl crush sensation again. The longest moments of my life were the time the cops stood at my front door on the night Mike was killed, but this morning, those two minutes my electric toothbrush demanded were a pretty close second as I itched to finish and head out in the car with Kylie. On the other hand, stinky hangover breath was no treat for either of us, so I stuck it out.

As I drove out towards Hall, the quaint little town on the

northern edge of the Australian Capital Territory, I pondered the kiss at breakfast. What did it mean? Had it been a hint of romance to come, or a friendly attempt to make me feel better about my own clumsy actions last night? Self-doubt pressed down on me like one of those machines that crushes up old cars, and I worried about how to handle the situation. Where was Lucille when I needed her? I had no idea what the next step should be, and I didn't want to make a dog's breakfast of it again.

I streamed a playlist I'd put together through the car player thing. I wasn't a guru at that, but I could get the music to play. The playlist had a lot of songs I thought were classics, along with tons of cheesy old songs I knew weren't great, but they brought me joy for this reason or that, memories, or just something joyous in the song itself. Kylie sang along with me, and of course, she had a stellar voice even if she did butcher the lyrics through not knowing the songs. I could never get into a relationship with this woman. I couldn't live with the constant sense of inferiority I'd have next to her.

"I like this music. It's varied and quirky."

"You don't find it too loud? I know loud noises bother you."

"Not as much now, honestly. At first, the sounds were painful, but remember, I'd spent endless cycles not hearing anything other than the Thought."

I turned it up a bit and we sang louder. I wanted to ignore the Hall turning and drive on, happy to spend time with Kylie, singing and laughing, but I could only take impetuosity so far. We parked the car and wandered the little town. We had a coffee in the café in the main street, then got back in the car. Hall is cute, but it's really small. I drove south and pulled off at

Cockington Green. Kylie was so taken with the large models outside the dinosaur museum, I gave in and bought two tickets. No kid ever walked around that museum in as much awe as Kylie, and she absorbed every detail. It took way too long, but at last I dragged her out, and we drove back to Belco and the mall.

She had expensive tastes, but if I'd had her body, so would I. It was worth every cent, even though I wouldn't have been caught dead in some of the things she liked. She could wear anything and make it look great, and when I suggested a bra, she said she felt awkward about having to work out the size of her boobs at her age. I told the woman Kylie had lost a lot of weight and wanted to make sure she got a perfect fit. I don't know whether the woman was on our team, but if she was, Kylie must have made her day.

"Our" team. I laughed to myself at that. Look at me, the dyed-in-the-wool lesbian, playing on the gay team like I'd always belonged. Maybe I had. Maybe I'd lied to myself all those years, but I didn't think so. I had been attracted to Mike when we were young, and I had never thought about women when Jo and Lucille had nagged me so much about getting back out there, it finally drove me to look for company other than the pair of them. Look where that got me. Rick. I laughed again.

I made pizzas. Kylie had tomatoes, capsicum, onions, and cucumber, which I loathe. Mine had some ham and cheese. Empathy be damned; pizza should have meat on it. We drank a bottle of wine and watched *The Notebook*, which made us both cry. At no point did a kiss from Kylie reappear, and physical contact was limited to the occasional kick in the thigh as one of us moved.

It had been a perfect day, although I resisted the temptation to say so to Kylie. We had done next to nothing, but I'd been in her company, which I hadn't expected to be when I got up that morning. We headed off to bed without even a goodnight kiss.

I didn't feel so guilty thinking about her as I touched myself, and I fell asleep with her face in my mind.

25

Jo rang on Sunday morning. I arranged to see her the following day, after I dropped Kylie at the library. She was surprised to learn Kylie hadn't gone home, and I had a hard time explaining it all as she probed and pried for any whiff of scandal or stupidity she could berate me about.

Sunday revealed another quirk of my unusual houseguest. We were surfing the television in the late afternoon when we came across a game of baseball from Seattle. I knew nothing about baseball, but Kylie stared at it so hard, I worried about that unblemished, unlined forehead. "I like this game. I like the way it progresses. There's so much tension. It's a team game, but at the same time there's a lot of individuality in each at bat."

She'd lost me at, "I like this game." She watched the whole thing while I read the book she'd consumed on that first day. After the game, we put some music on, and I continued my book while Kylie sat next to me and hummed along with the songs she liked.

To my surprise, she turned and lay down on the lounge, her head on the cushion and her knees in the air. After a few minutes, she stretched her long legs out across my lap. I played it cool, unshakeable, unfazed, more relaxed than James Bond with a laser heading for his groin. I carried on reading but dropped one hand onto her shins.

When I touched her, it electrified me. I felt a little tingle of excitement between my legs, but more than that flowed through me. The simple sensation of touching her legs bounced my heart up into my throat then down into the pit of my stomach before it settled in its usual place, galloping like a thoroughbred at the races.

Whenever I turned a page, I dropped my hand back, a little higher each time until it rested on her thighs. My poor old heart took another beating when she put one of her hands over mine, even though neither of us said a word. The mood in the room felt charged with tension for no real reason, to me, at least. I struggled to turn the page one-handed, loath to move my hand out from beneath hers.

She solved my dilemma. "Can friends do the shagging?"

I hadn't expected the bizarre question, and I lowered the book until it rested on her shins. I turned to look at her. Her earnest gaze burned into me. From anybody else, it would have been a ridiculous question, but from Kylie, it seemed as normal as going to the bathroom. "Of course. Why not?"

"Does it affect their friendship?"

Hmm. I puzzled over whether to give her the truth or lie to her in the hopes of luring her into bed. I couldn't do the dishonourable thing. What a numpty. "It can do, sure. Sometimes the relationship can go wrong, and it can destroy the friendship that existed before."

She nodded. "I wouldn't want that."

Damn. "*Never mind the friendship, woman. I want you like the night wants the morning to arrive so it can bugger off to bed.*" Or do I? I realised I'd be disappointed not to have her friendship. She'd been in the house for less than a fortnight, but I'd grown used to her, grown used to the company, the easy conversation, her curiosity about everything, the simple shared things we did together around the house and outside it. "Neither would I."

"Is it wise then? You are a fabulous friend."

"You've never had another friend to compare me to, you twit."

Small sparkles of laughter gambolled out of her mouth and glittered in the air between us. "I know, but you're still a good friend."

"Wow. I've lost my fabulous tag already? I'm only good now?"

Kylie swiped at me with one hand. Not the one lying on mine, I noticed with a triumphant half-smile. "Be serious. We need to think about this. I don't want us to make a mistake."

"*Girl, I've seen you naked. There's no universe in which sex with you would be a mistake.*" I managed a laugh. "What about that impetuosity you like so much?"

She smiled but said nothing. We looked into each other's faces like two poker players, each waiting for a tell from the other. "Tomorrow I'll read some books on the matter."

I pulled a face of disdain. "You're going to let a library book tell you whether or not to go to bed with me? Make sure you read, "*How To Be A Lesbian.*""

"There's no such book."

"How do you know, smarty-pants?"

"Because I've read the catalogue. No such book exists."

"Well, aren't you a bundle of surprises and chance pieces of trivia?" I sighed. "Kylie, if you don't want us to get involved, I'll understand." I wouldn't, but it seemed like the right thing to say, even though it would devastate me. I'd give up all my money, the house, the Benz, everything if I could make this woman my first—

I stopped the thought. I'd focused on wanting her to be my first time with another woman, but what if I wanted her to be the last, too? The thought shattered me. It couldn't be. Sooner or later, she'd have to go into Lake George and fulfil her stupid task, and she'd be gone. Could I deal with that? Should I even expose myself to the risk it would destroy me, break my heart into so many pieces, it could never be put back together? I'd already gone through enough hell with Mike. I didn't think I could take it a second time.

"I do want us to, Abi. I just don't want to lose your friendship."

I tried to contain my excitement. I'd reached whatever base this would be in the stupid baseball game she'd watched earlier, but I had no idea how to take the next, or whatever they'd called it. "Let's not rush it, then." Wow, that had been hard to say. I wanted to more than rush it. I wanted to tear those new Lycra pants off her and tug her into my bedroom. She looked so good in the tight pants, I could hardly keep my eyes off her, but she'd look pretty good out of them, too.

She squeezed my hand and didn't relax her grip much afterwards. "That's a good idea. I knew you'd understand."

I didn't, but I could pretend. I had a feeling she would be worth the wait.

26

On Monday morning, after I dropped Kylie at the library, I
wandered over to the tall building where Jo and Steve had their
unit. She let me in, and I rode the lift up to their floor. They
had a great view north over the lake, but the two-bedroom unit
felt a little small since Grace had come along. Steve worked
from home most of the time and had his desk and computer
gear in her bedroom, which made the room cluttered. Maybe
they could afford to move to a bigger place soon.

I could have helped, and Mike and I had paid off their
mortgage after we sold the business, but I'd always encouraged
her to stand on her own two feet where money was concerned,
and I didn't know how long I would have to make my own
money last. Besides, Jo hadn't asked for any help, and it was
usually best to wait until she did than risk death from a thousand stares by raising it with her. Either way, they'd both be set
when I died. Whether they'd move into the house in Carson
Street or sell it, I wouldn't care.

Steve popped out to say hello, then returned to his troll cave. Grace was colouring, which remained her current favourite thing to do. When I moved a folded stack of laundry to sit on the lounge, she abandoned her work and climbed onto my lap. She set her little face in an earnest look. "Grannie, where's the mermaid?"

Jo glanced up from the kitchen, where she made us both a cup of tea. "She's in the library, darling." I smiled at Grace and tried to ignore Jo.

"She's still around?" I could ignore Jo all I liked, but she hadn't ignored my answer, it seemed.

I didn't look over, focused on Grace. "She is."

Grace's own conversation hadn't ended. "What's she doing at the library, Grannie?"

"She's reading books, sweetie. She loves to read."

Jo's tone wavered between sarcasm and hatred. "They don't have books where she lives?"

I mean, should I? It tempted me to tell the truth and say they didn't have books in her home. I battled that side of me so hard, and I feel I'm owed some credit for that. I couldn't let it slide completely, of course. "That's none of our business, is it?" I included myself to take the curse off it a smidge and gave Grace a delightful smile into the bargain.

Jo put the two mugs on the coffee table and sat on the edge of a chair, leaning forwards as she spoke. "What's going on with her, Mum?"

"What do you mean?"

"I don't trust her. She's up to something."

Grace didn't agree. "I like her. She's funny."

I wrinkled my brow. I didn't think Grace and Kylie had talked much last week, but my granddaughter had taken a shine to the woman I wanted to... "*Focus, Abi.*" I glanced over to Jo. "That's just silly, darling. She's very nice. You don't know her, that's all."

"Neither do you, Mum. You met her less than a fortnight ago. How come you're so buddy-buddy with her?"

"That's none of your business. Don't worry, I won't be changing my will. You'll still get everything."

Stony silence. In all honesty, I deserved it. I don't even know where that came from, other than some resentment at the way Jo maligned Kylie despite the fact she knew nothing about her. I suppose my desire to be tumbling between the sheets with Kylie might have played into it. It was a horrible thing to say despite all that, and I felt remorse the moment the words left me. "I'm sorry, Jo. I had no reason to be rude."

"I'm not sure what to make of that little outburst." Jo picked up her mug and cradled it between her hands as she blew soft, cooling breaths onto the tea. Swirls of steam scattered around the room.

Grace to the rescue. "Grannie, what's a will?"

"It's something grown-ups do to make sure their family are looked after when they die."

"Are you going to die, Grannie?"

"Not today, I hope." I laughed and gave her a squeeze, and she threw her arms as far around my neck as she could get them.

"I'm glad. I'm going to do some more colouring now." She hopped off me and returned to her colouring book. I'd lost my ally and my barricade between her mum and me in one move. Curses.

Jo didn't waste any time now her daughter had left me exposed. "Well?"

I didn't grasp what she meant. "Well what?"

"What's going on between the two of you?"

How could she know? Had Kylie's sixth sense rubbed off on Grace and been passed along to Jo? I needed to stall for time. "What do you mean?"

"I mean why has a complete stranger been staying with you for two weeks? Is she threatening you to get money off you?"

I'm not sure whether my sigh of relief made any sound, but I heaved it anyway. Jo was barking up the wrong tree, thank goodness. "Not at all. She's a friend. She's good company, if you give her the chance, and I enjoy having her around." I would enjoy having her one day, I hoped, then felt guilty for thinking it.

Jo leaned back. I hoped that marked a downshift in her intensity, but you could never tell with Jo. She might be regrouping for another attack for all I knew. "What about the other one? What happened there?"

"She went somewhere else. She's travelling, and she'd seen enough of Canberra."

"I thought this Kylie woman wanted to get back to Lake George, or wherever she's from."

I'd had enough of the grilling. "Jo, none of this is any of your business. Why are you pushing so hard about it all?"

"Because you're my mother, and I have a responsibility to make sure you're safe. You're too gullible, and you're hopeless at setting boundaries."

"I don't need you to look after me. I'm a grown woman." The remark had irritated me, and I'm pretty sure my prickly tone left Jo in no doubt about it. Responsibility my arse, stupid girl.

"You're still gullible as hell."

"I've changed your nappies and wiped your shitty arse, Jo. I think you've over-estimated how much you need to look after me by some margin."

"I was just a child then."

"You're still just a child. Stay out of my business. Who I sleep with is my own concern."

Bugger. I'd got too mad and lost control. I'd over-stepped a boundary, which didn't make Jo right, but I'd confessed to more than I wanted to.

Jo's mouth hung open, her tea forgotten in her hands. Grace ignored us, thankfully, all her attention on not going outside the lines. A pregnant silence lay between Jo and me, fertilised with all manner of awkward offspring by the seed of my careless slip of the tongue. I wracked my brains for a way to correct the statement, to make it innocent without appearing to flounder for an excuse. Jo beat me to it. "You're sleeping with her?"

My derisive laugh sounded a touch too loud, even to my own ears. "Of course not. I meant that as a generalisation, as a suggestion you shouldn't poke into every little thing I do." Not bad, but would it convince her?

"What about Dad?"

Had she even heard my reply? "What about him?"

"How could you betray him?"

"*Ten thousand reasons, kiddo, most of which you know nothing about.*" I fought to focus on digging myself out of the hole Jo was hell-bent on making deeper. "I'm not betraying him. He's dead." That had been clumsy, and I'd implicated myself further. I should shut up. When you're already in a hole, it's best to stop digging.

"With a woman? How did you suddenly jump over to

women?"

"That's homophobic." Time to clutch at straws and see if one would keep my head above the water. I'd mixed my metaphors, and I felt a sensation I didn't enjoy; my throat had turned dry, my heart pounded in my chest, my hands shook. I was close to panic. I had to get a grip.

"No it's not. I just want to understand how my mother could be married to a man for twenty-five years—"

"Twenty-four." Why had I jumped in like that? What a stupid thing to say at a time like this. I almost slapped my thigh in frustration.

Jo's anger radiated from her face, her jaw set, her eyes narrow, her talons extended. I jest. "Twenty-four. How could you be married to Dad for all those years but now want to sleep with a woman? I don't understand it."

"I didn't say I wanted to sleep with her. I've explained why I said that."

"Grannie, are you angry at Mummy?"

I'd allowed my anger at Jo to become my sole focus. Grace shouldn't have to hear this argument, the rage and impatience in our voices, the harshness in our words. I smiled at her. "No, darling. We're just talking about the mermaid." I should leave before I ran out of straws or dug myself so deep, I'd never get out, depending on which metaphor I settled on.

"I like her." A child's simplicity. Why couldn't Jo be as uncomplicated as her daughter?

"So do I, sweetie."

"I'll bet you do." Jo's reply had been softer, more of a sarcastic mutter, really. "You only have to look at her to see that. Perfect figure, perfect skin—"

"Perfection is a societal construct. Stop making it a competition between her and you." I shouldn't have said that, because that was going to be red rag to a bull for Jo.

I was right. "A competition? What are we competing for? The affection of a mother who never really cared for me but has tumbled into bed with this supermodel-looking woman who's half her age in five minutes flat?"

"She's not half my age." Why did I keep regurgitating things other people had said to me? As soon as I said it, I knew I'd exposed my King. Checkmate, or as near as damn it. I'd refuted the age difference instead of the suggestion of sexual intimacy. She'd beaten me fair and square.

"Is everything okay in here?" Steve had appeared, a concerned look on his face. I presumed the raised voices had drawn him out of his cave.

Jo beat me off the start line. "Oh yes, everything's just hunky-dory. My mother is fucking a woman half her age. Never mind that my dad has only been dead for two years. She's moved on to greener pastures. A completely different shade of green, to boot."

"Ah." I'd always thought of Steve as an intelligent man, if a bit of a nerd, but that answer disappointed me. I felt sure he could have come up with something better. Live and learn, as they say. In the heat of the fire, he'd melted, and I didn't doubt he was wracking his brains for an excuse to back out of the room and return to the safety of computer geekery.

Grace giggled. "Mummy said a bad word."

More than one, if we're honest. I flashed her a smile filled with no confidence and no idea of the next thing I should say. So much nuance in one smile.

His daughter had given Steve the out he'd looked for.

"Come with Daddy, and bring your colouring book, Gracie. We'll leave Mummy and Grannie to chat."

What a bastard. Cunning, and beautifully played, I had to admit, but he should have stepped in, told his wife to stay in her lane, made some gay-positive statement, offered me another cup of tea, all the things a son-in-law ought to do. Instead, he'd waved a white flag and run for the hills under the covering fire of my bloody granddaughter.

I heard the door of Grace's bedroom close. He'd shut himself in behind his barricade and washed his hands of the whole affair. Jo's stare contained so much vitriol, it almost melted my face off. I shrugged. "Like I said, it's none of your business."

"It won't last."

I already knew that, but I couldn't work out how Jo did. "We'll see. If it doesn't, it doesn't." Another brilliant retort. *"Maybe I should try out for the Australian Olympic Repartee team. I wonder when they hold the qualifying heats."*

"I'm not homophobic."

"I know that."

A quiet truce poked its head up from behind the lounge, ready to duck down if the lead started flying again. I stayed silent. It had always been the best policy when Jo was a kid. If she got mad with me, I just left her alone. She'd stew on the wrong she thought I'd done her, and in time she'd work out where she had misinterpreted something I'd said or done, and all would be well again. For a while, at least.

"More tea?"

I hadn't drunk mine, but it had gone cold. I'd forgotten about it until Steve appeared. "Sure." She went into the kitchen, and I wandered across to the island bench, careful to keep it between us in case she was only regrouping. "I love you, whatever you think. You're the best thing to ever happen to me."

She snorted. "I was, until little Miss Perfect came along."

I sensed that had been a parting shot, not a full-frontal assault, and I let it slide. "I didn't tell you enough as a kid. I'm sorry."

She dunked the tea bags in the water, her attention anywhere but on me. "You didn't."

"Well, I'm sorry. I do love you, more than you can know."

"I love you too."

Jo turned to face me, tears moistening her eyes, ready to spill down her cheeks any second. She gave one of those teary laughs, the ones that have a quiver in the lips to suggest they're just a blanket someone has pulled over themselves to hide beneath. She put my mug in front of me, sniffed, and wiped her eyes with the back of her hand. "So, my stepmum is really called Kylie?"

"Yep." I left the tea where it was. I wanted my hands free for when she came round the bench and ran into my arms.

"Kylie what?"

"Yep." Her face wore confusion, and I realised I'd done it again, regurgitated the entire made-up name thing. "Watt. W-A-T-T."

Another teary laugh. "Seriously?"

"Seriously. What a bloody stupid name."

I liked this laugh more. It sounded genuine. "She's not so perfect after all."

"She's nowhere near perfect. She makes the worst tea I've ever drunk."

I was glad I hadn't picked up the mug.

We sat down again after a lengthy hug and chatted about Kylie, about the weather, about Grace, just mother/daughter stuff, and nobody would know how viciously we'd argued, but I had a heavy feeling in my chest. I'd outed myself, sort of, and taken credit for sleeping with a gorgeous woman when I hadn't actually done anything more than kiss her and hold her hand. I'd risked estrangement from my only daughter, and I'd thought uncharitable things about my late husband. At least I hadn't blurted my thoughts out to a daughter who loved him more than herself and missed him every day.

If I'd known coming out was this hard, I might have stayed in.

27

Soon after midday, I picked Kylie up and we walked to the car. I asked if she'd found, *"How To Be A Lesbian,"* and she laughed. "No, but I found a few books about baseball. The story of the integration of the Negro League into the Major League fascinated me. Jackie Robinson was a trailblazer."

I knew nothing about Jackie Robinson, but I knew plenty about the way white people have treated coloured people down the centuries, and none of it made me proud. A plane flew over, doubtless one of the many that flew the Sydney to Melbourne corridor every day, and Kylie glanced up. "Is that an aeroplane?"

I bent my head back to study it. "Yes. We call them planes though."

She stopped and watched it for a while as it left a long white gouge in the sky behind itself. "It's strange, really. Instead of leaving the animals of the air in the care of their own People, you have created machines so you can fly among them while you ignore or eat the animals you should be tending. You humans have made a complete mess of this."

I squinted at her, my vision blurred by the brightness of the blue sky above us. "So you'd never want to fly in a plane?"

She looked at me with half a smile on her face. "I didn't say that. What's it like?"

"I like it, but it scares a lot of people. It's nothing more than a metal tube you're trapped in for an hour or more while you're suspended ten thousand metres above the ground."

"The views must be spectacular." She spoke distractedly as she tilted her head again to watch the plane recede northwards.

"On a clear day, they are." An idea came to me, and it made sense, to me anyway. "Would you like to go up in one?"

Kylie fixed me with a stare loaded with questions. "Would I be allowed into it? Would I be safe so far up?"

I didn't hide my ironic laughter. "You'd be safer than anyone. If it fell apart, you could fly back down."

She frowned. "I'm not sure about that. Winona believed we could Translate as many times as we want, but my Guardians said once I went back into the water that would be that; I could never come out again."

"Why don't we go somewhere for a few days? Melbourne, maybe, or the Gold Coast. There are flights direct from Canberra. You could find out what it's like to fly, and you'd get to see a different part of the country."

"That might be fun." She smiled, and I turned into a melted jelly baby right there in front of her. "Would they let me into the plane though?"

"You couldn't fly internationally, but on a domestic flight you don't have to show any ID. I can make the booking and just add you as a second passenger." Her smile was torture. I wanted her to never smile again so I would never have to be so weak in the knees again, but I wanted her to never stop smiling so I could enjoy that heart-stopping sensation for ever.

"I would like that. Where shall we go?"

"The Gold Coast will be warmer. We can walk on the beach. I don't imagine you've ever walked on real sand."

"Only when I came out of the lake that day."

"That's a man-made beach. You need to experience a real beach that stretches as far as you can see." I decided to book the flights and a hotel once we got home. The argument with Jo had dampened my spirits, and I needed a pick-me up. Kylie seemed excited to fly on a plane despite her earlier mournful judgement on them.

When Kylie asked how my morning had been, I lied. I couldn't tell her I'd had a blazing row with my only daughter over her. I said Grace had asked about her, and she seemed pleased. "She's a cute little girl."

"Just like her grannie."

She looked sideways at me but said nothing. When we got home, I grabbed the iPad before she could monopolise it and booked two tickets to the Gold Coast on Thursday. I splashed out on Business Class even though the flight lasted no more than an hour and a half. It might be Kylie's only chance to fly, and I wanted it to be special, or as special as an hour and a half in domestic Business Class can be. I hadn't flown anywhere for a while, and I would enjoy the better experience too.

As we were preparing dinner, a thought came to me out of nowhere. "Why can't your People say your names here?" I remembered the faces Winona had pulled as she'd tried, and smiled.

Kylie looked down, her usual gesture as she pondered

anything. "I don't really know. I hear it in my head, but I can't get this body to pronounce it."

I stopped chopping the onion I'd been working on and gave the idea some thought. "Could you write it down?"

She frowned, as though she didn't care anymore that she might get a tiny line on her forehead. "I don't know. That's a good idea, though. Let's try it."

Kylie's eyes sparkled with excitement. It seemed she more than half-believed the idea might work, and I felt proud of myself. I didn't allow any mental space for the thought she might just write some gobbledygook nobody could pronounce as she knelt at the coffee table with the back of an envelope from some junk mail that had been in the mailbox that morning and a pen she pulled out of a drawer. I wondered whether she would instinctively know how to write. We were about to find out.

I sat on the lounge to watch. She stared at the paper, and her tongue protruded a little way out of her mouth in a perfect caricature of somebody who's studiously thinking about some tough academic task like the formula for splitting the atom, or writing their name. The pen scratched across the paper for at least five minutes, and I got bored. I picked up my book while Kylie continued with a job even Grace could have finished several times over by now.

At last, she heaved a breath, as though she'd just reinvented supersonic commercial air travel. "There."

I put the book down and took the piece of paper she proffered me. I looked at the arrangement of the letters she'd written. Of course, she had beautiful writing, neat, all in a straight line, perfectly legible. I teased her. "Tina Turner?"

"It doesn't say that, does it? That's not even close." My eyes must have betrayed me; that or my smirk. "Very funny." She laughed. "Try to read it out loud."

I gave it a go, tentative and anxious not to offend her. "Lukttaret?"

She chewed the inside of her cheek. "It's close, I suppose, but it's not right. Our language includes more than words and letters. Inflection, other sounds, pauses. I don't know. That's close, and that's all I can write in your letters." She gave her head one short, sharp nod. "Let me try Winona's name."

That took even longer. Her name seemed to be as thorny as she herself had been, like that came as a surprise. I half-expected it to be PainInTheArse when Kylie handed the envelope to me again. "Towbuniik? That's a bad name. It suits her, in a way. Difficult to deal with and bloody awkward."

Kylie laughed. "That's nowhere near right. Perhaps I wrote it wrong. I could try again."

"As tempting as that is, I may have to resign myself to living the rest of my life without knowing how to say her name. Such a shame."

Kylie's eyes twinkled. "As you wish."

"Dinner. Let's get back to it. Lukttaret." I creased my brow. "Yuk. I don't like it. Let's stick with Kylie."

Lucille rang that night. I said I'd told Kylie how I felt and denied her insistence we must have had sex. I couldn't mention the argument with Jo without the risk Kylie might overhear some of it, so I saved that for a more convenient time. I told her about the trip and refused to believe her when she said Kylie was sure to reward me for the tickets with a roll in the hay. I didn't want to believe it. Disappointment had become too familiar a companion recently, and I preferred to keep it at arm's length for now.

The next day, Rick's name popped up in my screen to take the edge off Christopher Cross's cheery ringtone. I debated not answering, and Kylie advised me not to, but I'm just not a "push the X button" kind of woman. "Rick."

"Hi, Abi. I've been thinking."

I bit my tongue and swallowed the insult about his thought capacity that sprang to my mind. More mixed metaphors. I'd become good at them. "About?"

"Last Friday. I think I over-reacted."

"No, Rick. You don't 'think' you over-reacted. You did over-react."

Short silence. He couldn't project contempt through a phone like Jo. Amateur. "I'm sorry. I'd like to see you again."

Kylie was watching me, curiosity and impatience in her green eyes. I longed to disappear into those green pools of mystery and be consumed whole by her. I dragged my attention back to Rick. "I don't think that's wise, Rick."

Another silence. He could, it turned out, project misery through a phone. I reassessed his projection status. Semi-pro, maybe. "Why not?"

"Well, let's see. I don't see any future for us. We're just not compatible. And there's Kylie too. As you know..." Oops. I'd gone too far and assumed something about my relationship with Kylie that was no more than wishful thinking at this stage, and in her earshot too. I felt my cheeks heat up as they reddened.

"I see." I hadn't expected him to use a line Kylie used all the time, but he had. "You're with her, then?"

I hoped she hadn't heard the question. "I am." A small pang of guilt jabbed into my gut. I'd used her as a convenient excuse to give Rick the flick. On the other hand, I wanted that excuse to be true so much now, I found it hard to focus on anything else, except her bum in those pants.

"I see."

I felt sorry for him. His voice was pure dejection wrapped in a blanket of despondency. I remembered how bad his jokes were and toughened up. "Well, thanks for calling, Rick. Have a lovely day."

"Bye, Abi."

I hung up. I felt like a jerk, but he really had been as boring as a power cut during a wet weekend. On the other hand, the conversation had made me think about my current infatuation with Kylie. Why did I have such a potent desire for her when I'd never considered a relationship with a woman before? It couldn't be as simple as her stunning looks and figure; that would make me as shallow as Lake George before the rains. I might be that shallow, but I sure as hell didn't want to think I was.

What did she see in me? I was forty-nine, a touch of salt and pepper in my hair, plain as Plain Jane with a side order of plain, robust—a lovely euphemism for overweight—in my one-hundred-and-sixty-centimetre frame. A hundred-and-sixty-five if I stood upright and on my toes a bit. I had old-fashioned tastes in clothes and music and drank too much wine. Not quite front cover of the fashion magazine material, whereas she was a centrefold. It made no sense.

Had I been drawn to her through some sense of punching above my weight? I didn't think so, although I was. Or rather, I would be, if I could get her to agree to my fantasies. It made no sense for me to have changed team this late in life. If I'd been bisexual all my life, I could see it. Had I repressed some part of myself throughout my marriage to Mike? Had it been some form of societal pressure? Marry well, do well in your career, push out a sprog or two, don't dream about wild, uninhibited sex with the best-looking woman on the planet.

I realised Kylie was looking at me in expectation. I'd been away with the fairies, and no doubt she had waited for an update on the Rick situation. I gave her the abridged version. We pottered through the rest of the day, and as we headed for our bedrooms, Kylie gave me another kiss on the lips.

28

I lay in bed and revelled in the ecstasy of the kiss. As far as closed mouth kissing every few days went, this relationship would have to be the best I'd ever been in. If I lived long enough, we might even reach the head-in-lap-in-front-of-the-television stage. I could hardly wait, but sleep couldn't wait for me to finish my dreamy fantasy, and I drifted off with the tingle of ten thousand volts of electricity still on my lips.

On Wednesday, we went into the garage, where no self-respecting Australian ever parks their car, not least because they're always cluttered to the gunwales with stuff. Man shed stuff. Discarded kids' stuff. Might find a use for that one day stuff. I'll get round to fixing that stuff. Stuff. I'd come to the garage not in search of this stuff, but on a quest for our suitcases, which lay somewhere among the stuff. I found them, covered in dust, one of them with some bird poo down one side. I gazed around as though I might solve the mystery of the bird that had done number twos on my suitcase, then shrugged as though some words from a mysterious, wizened old wiser elder had slaked my thirst for understanding.

A wet cloth soon took care of the thoughtless bird's leavings, and we both wrinkled our noses in disgust as we consigned said cloth to the garbage bin, never to sully our lives with memories of the incident again. Kylie had been excited to pack, but to be frank, her few clothes looked pathetic in the big suitcase, and we decided to squeeze everything into one and hope the Gods Of Short-Shipped Baggage didn't see our dull little piece of luggage as shinies they must have at any cost.

We were only staying for three nights, so I packed eight interchangeable outfits and four pairs of shoes. In the end, when I added a spare pair of just-in-case shoes, the case wouldn't close, and we had to go back to the two-suitcase solution. I put some of my underwear in Kylie's case. It might cast some charm on her clothes in the hold of the plane and lead me to get very, very lucky indeed, or it might mean nothing more than I'd have some clean undies if the afore-mentioned Gods spirited my case away to add it to their Smaug-asbord of illicit goods. I explained my pun to Kylie; she wasn't as impressed as I hoped, but I stored it up. Eat your heart out Rick, I've come up with a cracker here.

Kylie wanted to put some of her underwear in my case, but she barely had enough to get through the holiday, and we'd have to go shopping for more, so there didn't seem any point.

Thursday morning arrived, wet and miserable. I felt bad for Kylie. The low cloud would spoil the views, but maybe the weather would improve as we flew north. I drove us out for the flight. Hang the expense, and parking at our little airport is a breeze compared to the mega airports in Sydney and Melbourne. We'd checked in online, so we dropped our cases at the bag drop machine. Everything was new and exciting to Kylie, and she could barely contain her elation and wonder at each step of the process. As we approached the x-ray machines, I had a thought, and it worried me. I slowed my pace to turn it over in my mind.

What if she didn't show up on the machines? That would be awkward. I consoled myself with the belief none of us showed up, only the things we'd forgotten to put in the trays; small things like keys, phones, half-scale replicas of the USS Enterprise. The things people got sent back for never failed to amuse me. To my relief, Kylie went through first time, although from the looks on some of the security people's faces, she narrowly escaped a pat-down and a full cavity body search. I got pulled out for the explosives check on my carry-on, of course. If I was what terrorists looked like, then we were all safe and sound for the rest of time.

I resisted the temptation to whisper to the gawking man who swabbed my bag, "She's my girlfriend." It would have been fun, but I wasn't sure whether that was the kind of joke that would see me deported from the ACT in chains to some over-crowded prison in Sydney.

We went to the lounge, one of the privileges of flying at the sharp end. Of course, the lounge in Canberra isn't much better than sitting out in the terminal, which was never crowded or noisy and offered better food choices, although you had to pay to eat outside the lounge, I supposed. Kylie gazed out of the window at the bewildering array of planes outside and had to search Google for all three of them.

We obeyed the disembodied voice that told us to head for the plane and waited patiently in the Business Class line while people who weren't in Business Class pushed in ahead of the rest of the Economy crowd. My heart leapt into my mouth when a red light came on as Kylie swiped her boarding pass, but the gate attendant turned it the right way up, and all was well. We were aboard.

I gave her the window seat and said I thought the weather might clear up once we headed north. Kylie didn't care. She stared out of the window through the entire boarding process, pushback, and taxi. She jumped when the engines roared up to full throttle, or whatever it is, for take-off. I don't think she heard the flight attendant ask if she wanted a pre-departure glass of anything, but I took two glasses of bubbles and drank them both. Kylie didn't notice, and I laughed inside, one of those evil "Bwahahaha" laughs. "*Most cunning, Doctor Strangelucas.*"

I'm happy to report the weather came to the party. Somewhere north of Sydney, the skies cleared, and Kylie stared down in wonder at the scenery beneath us. I turned down the hastily served meal on her behalf; there was no vegan option anyway. She ordered another glass of bubbles vicariously through me and drank it in the same remote-controlled way. I was feeling a bit tight by now, but Kylie was having too much fun looking out of the window to be distracted by alcohol, so I took one for the team.

I'm not sure she enjoyed the landing. That bump when the wheels hit the ground and accelerate from zero to two hundred and sixty kilometres per hour can be a daunting moment when experienced for the first time, and the rapid deceleration seemed to alarm her, but I reassured her with a hand on her forearm, which I forgot to remove as the plane taxied to the terminal.

Strewth, it was hot outside the terminal. Not flesh-melting

hot, but compared to Canberra, it felt bloody hot to me. The air even smelled hot, although the aviation fuel might have had something to do with that. Fortune had smiled on us, and both suitcases and our entire collection of underwear had landed with us, and we took an Uber to Broadbeach. I'd only been to the Gold Coast a few times, but I preferred Broadbeach to Surfers; not as busy and with better restaurants. Again, I'd splashed out on a nice suite with a balcony overlooking the sea.

I suggested we should visit the local shops and buy her a swimming costume; cossie, as we Aussies say. She didn't look convinced. "What if I Translate in the sea?"

"You don't in the shower, so why should you in the sea?"

She turned to gesture out of the window. "Winona said we don't Translate unless we want to, but that's a lot more water than in the shower, and my People will be in it."

"They can't see you, can they? Isn't that what Winona said?"

She looked down, a trait I'd noticed in her whenever she wasn't sure of herself. "We can't see each other, but we can see the Uprights. We can see you."

I hoped she didn't hear my brain as the cogs turned, and I tried to figure out the implications. I couldn't understand it. "How can you see us if we're the same as you?"

"I don't know. Maybe because you no longer reside in the Balance. I can't understand it any more than you."

That was a given, really. I didn't understand a single bit of it, and at times I'd questioned my sanity. "How about we go to the beach, and you put your feet in the water? I'll hold your hand, and if you start disappearing, I'll pull you out. If you don't disappear with your feet in the sea, I don't think you will if you swim."

She agreed, but on the beach, her nerve failed her. I spoke in a calm, reassuring voice, told her everything would be okay, that I'd never let go of her hand. That was the best part of the plan, as far as I was concerned, of course. All the upside for me lay in holding her hand. What a baby I'd become. At last, she agreed, and put one tentative foot into the surf while I gripped her hand to reassure her. Sparks lashed up my arm from the touch of her skin, singed my flesh and burrowed into my heart. How had I become so infatuated in so short a time?

Kylie put both feet in, then laughed and tugged me into the water. Unprepared for the yank on my arm and still wallowing in my delirium at the feel of her hand in mine, I fell headfirst into the water. I knew I should have worn my cossie with a t-shirt over it or something. One outfit down, seven to go. I spluttered, spat water out, waved away her apology, then knocked her over into the incoming wave. We splashed around like two five-year olds for some time. Kylie's grin made all the expense worth it. If I could live my life again, I'd do everything the same just so I wouldn't miss the expression of unbounded delight on her face in that moment.

Drenched, we almost skipped back to the hotel. We sneaked in through the door that opened straight into the mall it adjoined and hid until a lift came. I thought they might throw us out if any staff members saw the state we were in, covered in sand and dripping water everywhere. It had probably been the best afternoon of my life.

29

We showered, threw our clothes into the bath, and got ready to head out for some dinner. We stopped in the bar for a glass of champagne on the way out, and Kylie added another entranced admirer to her charm bracelet. The poor young fellow behind the bar couldn't take his eyes off her. Her skin had already coloured a little from the sea, sand, and wind, and she'd begged me to help her curl her hair. She looked spectacular, and while he made it obvious he wanted to get cosy with her, I hid the fact I wanted it twice as much.

We wandered around Broadbeach and looked at numerous menus in restaurant windows until Kylie found one she liked the look of. A bottle of wine and a pleasant meal later, we headed to a nearby bar for another glass of champagne. I was more than a little drunk by now, and I reminded myself not to do anything stupid to ruin this day. Perfection might be a construct, but whoever had constructed it had done a decent job today.

I'd booked a room with a King bed, not thinking about the arrangements, and later that night, for the first time, I finally got to sleep with Kylie. That was all we did, although I did get another goodnight kiss. Twice in one week. Things were heating up between us. Just before I drifted off, Kylie whispered to me. "Abi."

"Yes?"

"Thank you."

I smiled and fell asleep with a vision of her cavorting in the surf, a beautiful creature beneath a beautiful sun in a beautiful sea, and now she lay next to me in bed.

She snored. She woke me up a time or two, but lucky for me, the booze soon took me off to sleep again. I didn't know whether to be disappointed at the rasping buzz of a chainsaw next to me, but I consoled myself with the thought I'd finally found a weakness in her I didn't have in me.

Kylie's words woke me in the morning. "You snore." Not the words anybody wants to hear when they wake up next to arguably the most beautiful woman in the world, and I turned my back on her in a huff.

"So do you. You sound like a tractor."

"I don't know what a tractor sounds like, but you're louder than that plane when we took off."

"You sound like ten tractors."

After a moment's silence, she laughed and pushed at me. "Get up. I want to go swimming again."

The hangover wasn't terrible, but it was bad enough, and I had no enthusiasm for an early start. "You've probably been swimming for billions of years. How can another hour hurt?"

"That wasn't the same. This is... Exhilarating. This body is cumbersome and hopeless in the water. Something else you've made a mess of, by the way. But it feels, Abi. I can feel the water, and the sand between my toes, and—"

"My foot in your bum if you don't shut up."

I relented and dragged my hungover, grumpy body out of bed. We didn't shower; if today went like yesterday, we'd have to shower later anyway. Kylie relented and let me buy her a cossie, so I put mine on with a tee over it. I stopped her buying the most revealing bikinis in the store. I just couldn't trust myself. She looked good enough to eat, and in all the good ways.

A t-shirt over her two-piece, she hopped and skipped beside me as we took the short walk to the beach and through the sand until we reached the flags. I explained to Kylie that while she could probably swim anywhere, in this body, she had to stay between the flags, and my old body definitely had to.

I asked her to put block-out on my back, and her hands as they ran over my body sent a firestorm of desire on a rampage through my entire being. I'd need to get into the sea quick smart before somebody noticed that one part of my cossie was damp while the rest wasn't. Kylie didn't think she needed to wear block-out, but to hell with that. I needed her to wear it, and the creepy thoughts I had while I rubbed it over her skin almost made me ashamed. Almost.

I'm not saying I put more on her than I should have done, but she could probably have flown into the sun and not been burned. Her back looked like one of those channel swimmers, covered with whatever foulness they slather all over themselves. I'm fairly sure some passing stranger wished he'd brought his skis so he could enjoy the pure white slopes of her shoulder blades. I cursed myself for dissuading her from buying one of the thong bikinis. I could have put block-out on her bum for the rest of the day if I had.

I had unleashed a monster. She showed no sign of ever tiring of the sea, and at one point she swam so far out, I got nervous. She swam like an Olympian, but she might swim out of her depth or she might encounter a shark. Poor shark. She'd probably blow it to the far side of New Zealand if it tried to take a nip out of that delectable flesh.

I lay on the sand and watched her frolic for a time. I couldn't stay in the water all the time like her. I needed a rest. I turned and tutted. One of the lifeguards watched her through binoculars. I couldn't blame him, I suppose. If someone did get in trouble in the water, they'd be safer with her anyway. She'd made the water hold that cyclist down; she'd probably make it spit a drowning person out onto the safety of the beach.

We ate at a different restaurant, then found ourselves at a bar where a few people were dancing to music that came from somewhere I couldn't determine. Kylie wanted to try dancing, but I resisted. I'd say I'm not much of a dancer, but that would do a disservice to people the world over who aren't much of a dancer. I look like a crab that's fallen onto the overhead wires of the tram, and that's when I'm in good form.

Kylie, naturally, was a natural. Not only could she bust any move better than the person who'd invented the move, the way her body moved, sensuous and seductive, meant I had to close my eyes for fear I'd jump on her and ravish her right there on the floor of the bar. Sexy didn't begin to describe it, and all the water in the sea couldn't have extinguished me if I'd watched her for an entire song.

We went back to the hotel, slept in the same bed again, and

I resisted her pleas on our last full day and insisted on a walk along the beach. "We can swim later. I want to go for a stroll."

We walked south towards Mermaid Beach. We chatted about everything and nothing. Kylie had to show off on some of the beach gym equipment that littered the path whenever we weren't on the sand. As far as I knew, she'd never worked out before, but I found it disheartening when she did twenty chin-ups or whatever they're called and only stopped when I said I was bored. She didn't seem the least out of breath, and I had to fight to keep my jealousy hidden. I couldn't manage one, and I fell in a heap when my hands slipped off the bar.

Kylie helped me up, and had the decency not to laugh. I dusted myself off, ashamed. How had I got into this state? It didn't matter about my weight, but I'd allowed myself to become sedentary and unfit. If I wanted to live a good long life, filled with adventure, great friends, and wild sex with Kylie, I needed to get fitter. "I need to work on my fitness."

Kylie nodded, which didn't help, if that had been her intention. "You should do something about it, then."

Damn. I'd harboured the faint hope she would wave some other-worldly limb over me, and I'd be Sally Pearson reborn, fit as a butcher's dog with none of the blood, sweat, and tears I'm sure Sally put in every day. "I could take up jogging." In the history of half-hearted propositions, that had been the half-heartedest proposition that ever got half-heartedly proposed.

Kylie smiled a full-hearted smile, inappropriate for the half-heartedness that half-filled me. "I'll run with you."

Based on the performance on the jungle gym or whatever they called it these days, it would be not so much with me as miles ahead of me. "If you leave me behind and I get a heart attack, I'll never forgive you. Especially if I die."

She laughed. "As if. I'll struggle to keep up with you."

I saw what she'd done there, and it cheered me up. "Thanks." I linked my arm through hers on a whim, and we turned back.

We swam again for a couple of hours when we got back, then had dinner. The goodnight kiss lingered longer than normal, and I wondered whether she knew how to kiss properly. I opened my mouth a little, and she copied me. Damn. All this time, she probably thought she'd been pashing me, and I could have taken things a step or two further if I'd wised up earlier.

How could I take advantage of somebody so innocent, they didn't even know about kissing with tongues? I'd talk to her about it when we got home. It might seem a bit forward while we were sharing one bed, and I didn't want to seem creepy.

Another Uber, another lounge, another flight that enthralled her, and we were back in Canberra. Three days had flown by like three minutes. I couldn't recall a happier holiday than the trip north, and I wondered whether another, longer trip might be good for us.

I rang Jo to let her know we were home safely, and she invited us round for dinner on Wednesday evening. I said I'd have to check with Kylie, and I'd get back to her, but I thought Kylie and Grace would be happy to see each other, so I couldn't see a problem.

I wondered about the apparent change of heart. A week ago, Jo had behaved as though Kylie might be some demon sent from the bowels of darkness to take advantage of me. She was right, in a way, but not the way she thought. Now she wanted us both to come to dinner.

I mentioned it as we sat on the lounge. Kylie was watching

a game of baseball. It didn't feature Seattle, who she seemed to have adopted because they were called the Mariners or something. "I'd like to see Grace again. She's fun."

How to appear concerned without revealing all Jo and I had said last Monday? "Jo might not be the best company. She can be cranky."

"I'm sure it will be okay." She watched the game for a bit and muttered a lot. "Nice play, damn it." "Come on, umpire. That was never a strike." "Get out, get out, get... Gah." Stuff like that. It meant nothing to me, but it seemed she had adopted another team, and they weren't doing well. "You're concerned."

I looked up from my book, surprised by her words. "I don't care. I don't even know which team is which."

She pushed at me. "Not about the game, silly. I know you told me not to use my sense of your emotions against you, but I sense you're worried about dinner with your daughter."

I lowered the book, chewed at my lower lip. "I don't think she likes that you're here. She's suspicious about everything. She's just worried about me."

Kylie yanked her head round at a roar from the television, and she sighed, then muttered something I didn't catch before she turned back to me. "Why is she worried?"

"I think she believes you and I are involved. Romantically."

"Did you tell her we are?"

I fiddled with the pages of the book. "I might have, by accident."

"If we were, why would she worry?"

I tried to ignore my frustrations, with little success. "Because I've never been with a woman before, and she can't understand why I would be attracted to one now, after all these years."

"I see." I'd grown to distrust those two little words. They usually meant she didn't see, and she was trying to figure it out. "Is it unusual for two women to do these things? The shagging and the kissing?"

"Not at all, but I've left it a bit late in life to decide it's what I want."

"Is it still what you want?"

"God, yes." Ensure brain is engaged before operating mouth. I knew the warning, but I'd ignored it again.

She picked up on the enthusiasm I'd failed to contain for the prospect. "So the only thing preventing it is my uncertainty?"

Wow, that had put me on the spot, and I didn't quite know what to say. "I suppose so." I felt dreadful as I said it, like it put all the pressure on her.

"I'm afraid to, in case you feel love. I don't know how to feel love. We've already talked about it."

I couldn't deny it. "We have."

"The two women in the book, Ashe and Ember, they said it to each other a lot. This makes me believe it comes when two people are together long enough. If you felt it but I couldn't, it might hurt you."

"It wouldn't matter to me." I'd said it, but I wouldn't have bet my bank balance on it.

"Let's test whether we can be together in this way, then."

Confusion reigned for me, even though she doubtless believed she'd made perfect sense. "How?"

She reached out for one of my hands. "Tomorrow, you will drive me out to the water, and I'll go into it." I must have gasped, because she gave me a sad smile. "Once I have done my task, I'll come out again. If I can come out, we'll do the shagging. If I can't..."

She hadn't needed to elaborate. I wiped at my eyes. Pollen count must have been bloody high or something. "Okay."

"It's best to find out now, before you feel the love. Don't you agree?"

I exhaled for so long, I ran out of breath and had to gasp for air. "I do, but I'm scared. When I first read that book, I was surprised by how much they had sex, and how in love they were. I didn't think I could ever understand so much intimacy and devotion between two women. Now, it's all I want. If you stay, it's not a question of whether I'll love you. It's only a matter of when. If you go in and can't come out..." I had to stop and reach for a tissue. I blew my nose nice and loud, perfect for those intimate romantic moments, wiped at my eyes with my hands.

"It will only be worse afterwards. I must perform the task I have been given."

"I understand. It sucks, but I do understand."

"I will sleep in your bed tonight, but we mustn't do anything. Tomorrow, we'll test Winona's theory."

"Christ, I hope she's right." I didn't know whether I'd just thought that one or said it, but I didn't care, because I did hope she was right, with every atom of my being.

I got a long goodnight kiss, and I took advantage of it and used my tongue. I lay with Kylie wrapped in my arms until she got so hot, the sweat from my body had soaked the sheets, then I pushed away from her and turned over. Tomorrow would be the most important day of my life. How had I arrived here? I didn't know, but I didn't want to think about it tonight.

Tonight, I was terrified.

30

We ate some toast in silence. I didn't know how Kylie felt, but my bowels weren't giving me any confidence. I don't think I've ever been so afraid of anything in my life. When they came to tell me Mike had been killed, I had faced a future without the man I'd spent the last twenty-four years with. I had no idea what to do without him. It wasn't that he was my soulmate, the loss of whom shattered me and spread the pieces around the cosmos. I'd just done everything with and around him for so long, I'd got used to it. That had been a piece of cake compared to this. This test of whether Kylie could come back out of the water would define the rest of my life. For whatever reason, I'd become crazy about her, and to lose her now might really shatter me and spread the pieces around the cosmos.

I sighed and picked up my keys. "Let's do this. No point putting it off." So much unsaid in those eight words, but if I tried to say it all, we'd be here until next week.

We set off, and Kylie held my hand in silence as I drove

through Mitchell and onto the Federal Highway. We'd just passed the Bungendore turnoff when Kylie blurted out, "Stop. Turn around."

I'm a careful driver, but I risked a quick glance at her. "What?"

"I can't do it. I'm afraid. If I can't come out, you'll be devastated."

"We know that, Kylie. We agreed it would be better to find out before I fell for you completely."

She sat in silence for a kilometre. "I would be devastated."

I sighed. "You don't know how you'll feel. You may not even remember me when you Translate." That still wasn't the right word, but that seemed irrelevant at that point.

"I remember you now, and I don't want to forget you. I don't want to take that risk."

"Christ, Kylie. You don't make things easy, do you?"

"I'm sorry, Abi. I can't do it. Not yet. I like you too much."

"You're killing me, Kylie. It will only be worse if we wait. You know that. We talked about it last night." *Shut up, Lucas. She's offering you more time with her, and you're trying to talk her into diving into a lake she might never come out of. Are you some kind of idiot?*"

"I don't want to go into the water until we've done the shagging."

A bead of sweat trickled down my forehead into my eye. I wiped at its salty sting and shook my head. "You want us to have sex? Now? Before you go into the lake?"

"Yes. Turn around."

I didn't drive across the median, but I thought about it.

31

We got up when it was dark, hungry for something other than each other. Neither of us had any experience in the art of love between two women, but we both knew what we wanted and worked it out together.

As I dressed, filled with a warm glow of satisfaction I'd never experienced with Mike, I wondered why I hadn't switched to this team earlier. Kylie seemed bashful now we'd finally done the deed, and she giggled whenever she made eye contact with me. It would be fair to say I was pretty happy with my afternoon.

The next day, I washed the sheets from the bed Kylie had been using and put them away in the linen cupboard. I couldn't imagine we'd need them again. We hadn't slept much and got up way too late. I felt like a teenager, but I couldn't be bothered to look for one. Another gem of a joke. Abi Lucas, peerless comedienne. Besides, I was happy with the billion-years-old woman I had, thanks.

Late afternoon. Lots of lip chewing, nervous hearts pounding, heavy sighs. Dinner with Jo had us both concerned for different reasons. I couldn't understand why she'd had this apparent change of heart. Kylie worried Jo didn't like her, which would make her so nervous she'd make a mistake in the story about her past, which wasn't even much of a story anyway. I told her to be vague and mysterious, but I didn't have a lot of confidence in her acting ability. She hadn't had enough time to acclimatise to the humans' easy competency at deception and misinformation, despite her success with the woman in the library.

I decided to drive so I couldn't drink. Jo wouldn't have to deal with her mother getting drunk, and I wouldn't have to deal with my tongue, which tended to run its own race when I got on the grog. Jo buzzed us up, and we held hands in the lift like two nervous teenagers about to tell the girl's father she's preggo.

I wouldn't be getting on the grog, but it was immediately obvious Jo would, and in fact had made a substantial start on the process. Her slurred words shot out too fast and too loud, her cheeks shone like two rosy, red apples, and she roared with laughter at everything that could be considered even remotely humorous. Her intoxication did nothing for my nerves, and I worried about why she'd got so drunk so early. She didn't usually drink a lot, and even less since Mike had been killed.

Kylie accepted a glass of wine, but I stuck to water. Not even a mouthful of alcohol could be trusted in my blood tonight; Jo was drunk enough for all of us, and I was taking no chances on my own self-control. Steve looked embarrassed when he had to take over the cooking. They'd made pizzas, mostly non-veggie, but they'd made a smaller one Steve assured us contained only vegan ingredients. I mightn't have trusted Jo, but I flashed Steve a grateful smile. He was a nerd, but he was a kind nerd, and I doubted he'd have tried to pull a fast one on Kylie.

Grace didn't seem to notice. She went into ecstasy mode when she saw Kylie and pulled her over to her colouring books, where they lay on the floor together staying inside the lines and talking in hushed tones, something I'd never seen Grace do before. When Kylie glanced up, I gave her a reassuring smile. It didn't reassure me, but I can't say what it did for Kylie. At least she had something to distract her and a legit excuse not to interact with the drunken daughter.

Steve put all the pizzas on the table. Some re-arranging of chairs was required so Grace and Kylie could sit next to one another, and I offered a silent prayer to the non-existent gods Jo wouldn't throw a jealous hissy fit and claim Kylie had tried to steal her daughter. Grace insisted on a piece of Kylie's pizza, then complained it didn't have any cheese on it. Steve tried to explain, but it made no difference; Grace had decided mermaids just didn't like cheese, and science wasn't going to cut it against the imagination of a three-year-old.

Jo leaned forward as though we were so far away we might struggle to hear her otherwise. "So, how are you both getting on?"

I answered. "Good, thanks." I turned to Steve. "Hope you've got plenty of work."

He gave a humble brag kind of laugh. "Too much, actually."

"He never stops working." Jo waved a hand in the air that could have been a nag, a resigned acceptance, or to signal the start of a duel to the death between us all. "I'll bet you never stop either, hey Mum?"

I've always thought there are three levels of embarrassment. Mild, like when you fart in a lift full of strangers, Moderate, like when your foot slips off the brake, and you rear-end a cop car, and Severe, like when your drunk daughter cracks an off-colour joke about your sex life being as active as a warren of rabbits who've just found out the future of rabbit-kind depends on them procreating in enormous numbers, perhaps of multitudinous proportions.

Kylie focused hard on her pizza and some inane subject Grace fortuitously distracted her with. Jo stared at me as she raised her glass halfway between the table and her mouth. Steve coughed, and I felt for him. It must suck to be him at that moment, but he had it easy compared to me. Kylie's silence had hung me out to dry, and I had to find some response. "There's no need for that kind of comment." It wasn't my best work; I once called someone the "C" word when they insulted me, and this reply could only be described as tame by comparison, but in my defence, Kylie had distracted me from training for the Olympic Repartee team try-outs.

"Do you do it in my bed?"

Things had gone too far for Steve. "Jo—"

She cut him off with a wave that was as precise as her last one had been ambiguous. "Do you?"

I'd had enough. "It isn't your bed though, is it? Your father and I bought it, so it's ours."

"He's not around to claim his half of it but, is he?"

"Then it's mine. Until I decide otherwise, it's not your bed."

Steve stuck his head above the trenches again. "That's enough, Jo."

She parroted his words with a belligerent, sarcastic tone.

"That's enough, Jo. I'll decide when it's enough, okay?" She glared at him, and I can't deny my relief that he'd taken over as her main opponent and given me a chance to take a breath and calm myself down.

It didn't last. She turned her disintegrator rays back to me. I normally call them eyes, but tonight... "I don't want a stepmum, especially one called Kylie, for Christ's sake."

I leaned back in the chair, took a breath, glanced at Kylie, who had decided to ignore Grace as things heated up, and took a moment before I replied. "Tough shit, kiddo. You don't get to decide what I do with my life, and you definitely don't get to decide what people's names are."

Jo flicked her destructo-gaze at Kylie. "What do you see in her?"

I stepped in. "That has nothing to do with you. What the hell is wrong with you, Jo?"

Kylie, it turned out, could speak for herself. A woman who possessed such a skill. Who knew? "Your mother is a wonderful human being." I winced; can't deny it. Too close to the wind with the human being stuff there, Kylie. "She has a heart of gold, she's funny"—that was a lie, I think—"caring, and gentle. She's a beautiful person, inside and outside. And she's great in bed. In fact, I think we should leave, go home, and I'll let her fuck my brains out in your fucking bed."

You could have cut the silence with anything really: a cucumber, a plastic elephant from a tourist gift shop, an odd sock you found behind the washing machine, covered in dust bunnies. It was that kind of silence. Shock is too small a word for it. Kylie's reply even shut Jo up for a heartbeat. It was a majestic moment, and I thank the cosmos I didn't miss it.

Jo's red cheeks turned redder, that furious red that

suggested you should call the firies in case the curtains caught fire from the heat in her face. Unfortunately, she turned it all towards me. "You wouldn't be with her if she didn't look like that. You wouldn't be with her if she looked like you."

Jo had never been an easy person to know. If she'd been Lucille's daughter, I wouldn't have had anything to do with her. I hope Grace doesn't turn out like her mother, or her grandmother, for that matter. I hope Grace grows up sweet and kind and considerate. Despite Jo's thorny temperament, this night had been a whole new level of ugly, and I was done. I stood up, kissed Grace and Steve, held out a hand to Kylie. She took it, and we left. Didn't say goodbye, didn't fire off any parting insult, didn't call Jo the "C" word, although she deserved it. We went down in the lift, got in the car, and drove home.

I closed the front door, turned round, slid down it, and burst into tears.

32

Kylie helped me up, half-carried me to the bedroom, undressed me, and put me between the sheets before she slid in next to me. She wrapped me in her arms for a while, but she soon got too hot for me. It was like sleeping with a furnace, as though her body temperature needed to be higher than normal to sustain life. Combined with my perimenopause, which was kicking my arse these days, it was more than I could bear. I rolled away and told her I was hot.

"I'm not surprised. She was horrible to you. I'm sorry, Abi."

I laughed inside at her misunderstanding but rejected the notion of letting her know. "It's not your fault."

"I think it is, in part. She only got so angry because of me."

"Don't blame yourself. She had no right to say any of the stuff she said. She was drunk." Jo had been drunk, but I didn't believe that excused her atrocious behaviour. After the last argument, I'd thought we would be good about the whole Kylie thing, but she must have trodden on a big box of Lego bricks for her to be as angry as she was earlier.

I had a miserable night, tossing and turning all night, sleeping in fits and starts. I woke tired, despondent, and angry. Kylie wasn't next to me; she always woke early and just got up to read something on the iPad. I lay in the bed and replayed the night in my mind. Had I said or done anything to trigger the outbursts? I couldn't think of anything. I'd have to buy Kylie her own iPad. Unsure why that random thought had entered my mind, I tried to return to the disaster last night had turned into.

I could lie here and think about it all day, but it wouldn't make it unhappen. Not sure that was even a word, I sighed my weary carcass out of the bed and into some track pants and a t-shirt. Kylie looked up from the iPad and gave me a welcoming smile that sort of did make me feel welcome. "Morning." She could speak one simple word and make the horrors of the world disappear, as though her voice alone placed wards on the doors and windows and kept us safe.

"Tea?" I filled the jug. After last night, I needed my own tea. Not that Kylie's was toxic, it was just crap. For some reason, she couldn't get it right, either too strong or too weak, too much milk, or she forgot the milk altogether. I could make a magnificent cup of Earl Grey, then she could take the next tea bag out of the box and somehow make it taste like heartbreak, cars that won't start, and super-glueing yourself to the fridge.

I sat next to her on the lounge and got the important stuff out of the way. "I would like you even if you looked like me. I enjoy your company, and you're smart, funny, gentle, and caring. Apart from last night. Where did you learn language like that?"

Her cheeks coloured and her face covered itself in her embarrassment. "Social media. I'm on the Facetube."

I let that run around in my mind to see if it could find the correct corner to settle in, but no luck. "Facetube?"

She pushed and prodded at the iPad, which didn't complain, so I presumed it had escaped unscathed. "Facebook. Sorry."

"Oh." It still didn't quite fit in its corner. "How did you get on Facebook?"

"I created an account. I learned how to do it on the Google."

"It's just Google. Not 'the Google.'" Hadn't I told her that already?

"Are you okay? After last night, I mean."

She laid a sympathy hand on my arm, and I took the hand, intertwined our fingers. "Not really, but I'll get over it."

After a pause, she said what we were both thinking. "I hope she has a bloody awful hangover."

I couldn't stop the laughter, even though I felt ashamed we had been so unpleasant. "Me too."

A sparkle in her eye got my hopes up, but I'd misread it, and she had other things on her mind. "What shall we do today? I think we've earned a treat after last night."

She was right. We had earned the right to spoil ourselves. "Let's go into the city, have a massage or something, go shopping, and have a nice lunch."

The idea landed well, and we spent a pleasant few hours in the city centre. The massage soothed away some of the heaviness from my heart, though it returned that evening. I tried to take an interest in the baseball game Kylie watched, but I've never been much of a sports fan. She said it was early in the season and something about pitchers' arms, or was it bowlers? Anyway, she seemed happier with the way tonight's game had gone, and I finished the tale of Ashe and Ember. I saw everything through a new lens now I'd joined the team, and I found the sex scenes far more appealing. I suspected some of the things Kylie had done that first night had come from the book, but we'd already learned so much about each other it didn't matter anymore.

Lucille rang on Friday and wanted to meet for coffee the next day. Kylie seemed keen to meet her again, and Lucille offered to come to Belco rather than us have to go into the city again, so why not? Other than Kylie, I'd had nobody to vent to about Wednesday night yet, and Lucille would listen, empathise, and take my side. Afterwards, she would buy Plasticine, make a voodoo doll of Jo, and stick pins into it. She was just that kind of friend.

We met in a little café opposite the shopping mall and, as expected, Lucille got fighting mad. I'm not sure which she got angriest about: the argument itself, or the fact Jo hadn't rung to apologise yet. I pointed out I hadn't called her either, and if I wanted to restore some peace, I could be the bigger woman and take the first step. Her colourful language made me laugh, and I hoped Kylie hadn't tucked any of it away for her next meeting with Jo.

The coffee with Lucille opened a door in my mind I couldn't close again. Grace. Unless I found a way to smooth things over with my daughter, I might not see my granddaughter again. I talked it over with Kylie later in the afternoon, and we agreed I should call Jo. I didn't want any confrontation again, so I decided to play it cool, act as though nothing had happened, and we'd all had a lovely evening.

She didn't answer. I hadn't expected that, so I sent a text asking her to call me. To my surprise, she replied almost straight away. She'd rejected my call; ominous.

Don't want 2 talk 2 u

Why not?

Still mad at u

You're mad at me? You don't think it's you who was out of lone at all?

Bugger. Typo. I'd meant "line."

Y do u spell every word its so yesterday

That stung. I was only forty-nine, but my daughter had already left me behind in tech. Grace would grow up speaking a language I couldn't understand. I showed Kylie, who thought it was just Jo being a dick.

ur a dick

well eat a bag of them

I had to get Kylie to translate that. It seemed she'd learned a lot from the Facetube. My instinct was not to respond, Kylie's was more colourful. I settled on a compromise.

I'm your

Backspace, backspace, backspace, backspace.

I'm ur mum. U can't just ignore me

Try me

I sighed. I had no appetite for another argument, and I certainly wasn't going to do it in text, which made pidgin English look refined. I couldn't bring myself to insult her with, "f u ur a btch and i h8 u." Mrs Davis, my old English teacher would probably turn in her grave.

Call me when you're ready

dont hold ur breth

"Breth?" I couldn't decide whether that was textspeak, a typo, or I'd failed her miserably during her school years. I looked up at Kylie. "Wow. She's really mad."

"Her loss." Kylie snuggled in. Apparently, the game was so exciting, I couldn't persuade her to come to bed and wipe away all my frustration at my daughter.

The days passed, and still no word from Jo. I missed Grace, and I missed Jo. I voiced a plan to just turn up, but because she lived on the eighteenth floor, Kylie said Jo could just ignore me, and I couldn't get up to her floor to get into her unit.

Rick called though, the person I least wanted to hear from. I admired his tenacity. He was probably bored stiff with himself and wanted some different company. I politely turned down his offer of dinner.

A few days later, Kylie expressed some concern about the financial situation. She felt guilty because she didn't contribute anything and lived off my money. I didn't care. "Don't worry about it, honey. I've still got plenty stashed away. We'll be okay for a long time yet."

"Could I do some kind of work?"

I thought about it. "I don't see much call for people who can move water about and drown people in lakes. Unless you could get in touch with organised crime."

I should have known Kylie would take me seriously, and it took quite a while to persuade her what a hopeless idea it would be. "You could look into something to do with the environment, but you have no identification or TFN, so I don't know how you could get a job."

"TFN?"

"Tax File Number. You need one before you can work." I didn't like the look in her eyes. "What are you thinking? Don't even think about doing anything shady. I'm still a registered CPA, and if I'm caught with any hint of wrongdoing, I'll lose my licence. If we do fall on hard times, I'm the only one who can work, so don't bugger things up."

She held up her hands in a placatory gesture. "Okay, keep your hair on." Another phrase she'd picked up from somewhere.

We started jogging, and it killed me the first few times, even though we drove down to the lake and ran on the almost flat paths around it. "*Give it time, Abi.*"

It had been five or six weeks since Kylie came out of the lake when I first realised she hadn't had a period. I suppose I'd been expecting her to ask me about it, and she hadn't. As far as I could see, there could only be three explanations: she was hellishly late, something about her transformation from whatever she had been to human form meant she wouldn't have to cope with that bloody awful curse every month, or I had got her pregnant. I didn't think I'd made her preggo, although I'd given it a red hot go over the last weeks. She might be late, but I suspected something about her was incomplete, and in a good way, in this case. How could we find out?

I raised it with her, and she agreed with me. Kylie suggested I should cut her and see if she bled, and she laughed when I told her periods weren't the same as bleeding when you're cut. "It's just a way to test for normal human function, silly."

Nervous, I took one of my sharp knives from the kitchen. Kylie pulled her shirt up and suggested I should cut her side, above her hip bones where it wouldn't show much if she scarred. I held the knife near her, anxious in case I slipped and killed her. That might have been an extreme outcome, but I'd never cut anyone with a knife on purpose before, and it's not like the movies, I can vouch for that. It's scary, or it was for me. At last, I closed my eyes and pushed the knife blade into her flesh. She cried out, and I opened my eyes, begging for her forgiveness. When I pulled the knife out, it left a small gash at first, and a trickle of blood came out, but her flesh healed itself straight away. No scar, almost no blood, nothing.

I stared into her eyes. "Shit. You're invincible."

"That's good to know."

"Is it? What if you get hit by a bus? You'll just bounce back up like nothing happened. People will notice, and those people will want to know why."

"This cut is a small thing. We don't know about something as drastic as being hit by a bus."

"Well, I'm not standing by to watch you throw yourself under a bloody bus, so we're just going to have to make some assumptions about that."

"Does that mean I'll never get sick? I'll never need a doctor or anything?"

It hit me like a ton of bricks dropped from a great height. "You lucky cow. You'll never have to go to the dentist." She flashed her perfect teeth in a mocking grin. "Piss off. I hate you."

I'm scared to death of dentists. I go twice a year, and it petrifies me. That's why I'm so fussy about the two-minute electric toothbrush. When Jo gave birth to Grace, even if it had been three in the morning and an emergency C-section, I would still have taken two minutes to clean my teeth. I never want another filling or extraction. I never want to drool soup out of one side of my mouth because of that anaesthetic ever again.

"What's it like, the period?"

"Shit. It's like a shit sandwich, only it's shit spread between two layers of shit. You don't know how lucky you are. I don't miss them one bit. They're hell."

"Do you suppose I'll age, or will I always look like this?"

I'd have to teach her about discretion. It almost broke my heart to think she'd still look this way in twenty years, while I'd be wrinkled and stooped, and everything that didn't hurt wouldn't work anymore. That's when it hit me that in twenty years, she might not be here. She might have gone into the lake and not been able to come out again.

I think that was when I realised I'd fallen in love with her.

33

I told her, straight out. She did her looking down thing, like she always did whenever she thought something over. "I wish I could say the same, but I don't understand how to be in love."

"We knew that would be the case." I think I did a great job of hiding my disappointment there. We had discussed it, but it hurt like hell to find out we'd been right, and she couldn't feel the same depth of emotion I felt.

"Don't be sad, Abi. Tell me how it feels. Maybe I feel it, but I don't know it."

How could I explain love to her? I didn't think I could explain it to myself. I had to give it a try though. I couldn't believe how desperate I was to hear it from her now I'd said it. "I think about you all the time. If you aren't here, it's like I'm missing a limb. There's no universe in which I could imagine myself not sitting on the lounge reading while my heart smiles every time you growl at some baseball player who hasn't done what you wanted him to. At night, I can't see the stars because you outshine them; during the day I can't feel the sun because your warmth is wrapped around me. I love you." I felt a bit mushy, to tell the truth. "That's the best I can do."

She looked down again. "I don't know how to feel those things. I'm not saying I don't feel them. I just don't know whether I do or not."

I conjured up a brave smile despite my terror. "It's okay. As long as you're here, that's enough for me." It was almost true, but I'd give my left tit to hear those three little words, damn it. Okay, that was the one with the scar from that time Jo bit me, but it's still a hell of a sacrifice, and all for three words, eight letters.

The phone rang. I glanced down, looked up at Kylie, and pulled a "what do I do?" face. Jo.

"Answer it, you idiot."

I took a deep breath. A Mariana Trench deep breath. Then I pressed the green button. "Hi darling." Too chipper? It sounded squeaky and phoney to me. Maybe I was being too hard on myself.

"Grace wants to see you and the fucking mermaid."

"That's nice. I miss her. I miss you too."

Silence, but the thinking kind, not the "hope you've had your last meal" kind. "She misses you too."

"How's Steve?"

"Busy, as usual. Lunch tomorrow?"

I bit my tongue. I could take the moral high ground when I vented to Kylie later. For now, I didn't want to set Jo off. I didn't want to destroy this moment. "That would be lovely. I'll pay."

"Who cares who'll pay, Abi? Get a grip."

"Spending my inheritance now you've cut me out of the will?"

I looked to Kylie for some support. Whatever she saw in my face, I don't know, but she blew me a kiss. "Don't be silly, Jo. Steve paid for breakfast last time. It's my turn."

"What time?"

"Why don't we pick you up around twelveish? We can go out to one of the vineyards, maybe. Bit of a drive, but they have lovely food."

Another thinking silence. "Tell the mermaid to sit in the front. Grace is my daughter, and I'm not about to let her absorb your little plaything as a surrogate mother."

I had to clench my fist at that. I guessed there was still a lot of bridge-building ahead of us, but this would be a good start. I couldn't let it completely slide though. I couldn't betray Kylie like that. "Her name's Kylie, and she's not a mermaid. We'll see you tomorrow. Love you."

I waited. She hesitated, and I felt it, but she hung up without responding. I gave Kylie a weak smile, although I'd come to realise she was as strong as an elephant. "Lunch tomorrow. It's a start, right?"

Kylie folded me into her arms and kissed the side of my head, above my ear. "It is. I'm glad."

I drove down to Jo's building the next day, and Kylie and I got out together to ring the buzzer. It was my idea, to show Jo I'd go so far to meet her over this stupidity, but there were some concessions I wouldn't make.

When Jo and Grace came down, Jo stopped and stared through the glass doors of the lobby at us. Grace walked ahead of her to the door, then turned to look at her mum when she couldn't open it. I don't know what went through Jo's mind, but something crossed her face, and for a moment I thought she would turn around and go back up in the lift. Common sense must have prevailed, and she pulled the door open.

Grace ran straight to me, thank goodness, and threw her arms around my legs. "Grannie." She'd shouted it so loud, Steve had probably heard it up on the eighteenth floor. I crouched down and hugged her. She smelled of soap and little kids and innocence, and I buried my face in her mass of brown curls. I hadn't realised how much I'd missed her. I held her a bit too long, because I wanted my tears to stop before I gave Jo the satisfaction of seeing them.

I stood and took a step towards Jo. "Hello, sweetheart." I leaned in for a kiss, and there was a moment of awkwardness as she tried to avoid it, and it landed on her cheek, sort of. She pulled back and called Grace over to her. She clutched one of the little hands in her own, a clear message that Kylie was on the outer as far as hand-holding duties were concerned.

I drove out past Hall towards Murrumbateman, where there are lots of vineyards. It was a pleasant drive, not spoiled by much conversation. Jo's terse answers reminded me of Kylie that first day, when the only words she knew were the ones I'd already said.

During lunch, I asked Jo whether she could be a little less taciturn. For the first half hour, the only conversation that didn't involve Grace was the discussion of what food we all wanted and a short reflection on the pleasant setting of the vineyard between Kylie and me. At first, I thought she would explode into another fit of temper like at the dinner, but she took a breath and asked what we'd been up to.

I had to skate a little carefully on that. I didn't want to set her off again with a blow-by-blow account of my newly active sex life. "We've been doing a bit of shopping, and we had dinner with Lucille a few nights ago."

Jo nodded, and Kylie seemed to think I'd been short on detail. "Your mother has taken up jogging. She's trying to lose weight."

"She's got a lot to lose." It hurts when your own daughter says something like that about you, but I couldn't deny it.

"I've lost some already." I tried not to let any pride creep into my voice, but I'd lost almost two kilograms. Not much, but it was a start. Lots of starts going around at the moment, it seemed.

Jo stared at me. "Really? I hadn't noticed."

Kylie squeezed my thigh under the table. She'd only been a human for six weeks, but she seemed to have more idea of manners and decorum than my twenty-four-year-old daughter. "What about you? Been doing anything exciting?"

She shook her head. "Not much. Steve has been working. We've been getting on with our lives."

Had I detected a little barb there? Had she meant to imply she could fashion a life without her mother in it? Perhaps I'd been too sensitive. "We're thinking of taking a holiday somewhere warm."

"Nice. I don't think you've ever taken us on a holiday."

"You've never asked."

Kylie jumped in, perhaps sensing some tension. "Come with us. It sounds like Steve could use a break from work, and I think Grace would love the beach."

I didn't want to slap her around the face because I don't think violence solves anything, even a severe case of foot-in-mouth disease. Of all the stupid things she could have said, that one must rank as the stupidest. What had she been thinking?

"I'll talk to Steve about it. You're right. He needs a break before he kills himself."

I sneaked a quick look in a nearby mirror to make sure I hadn't died and fallen under the table, leaving Kylie and Jo with no alternative to becoming insta-besties. Last night, Kylie had been the "f-ing mermaid," now she could talk Jo into a trip with us by invoking Steve's over-working geekiness? It beggared belief. I decided to leap in and seal the deal. "That would be lovely. Where would you like to go?"

"The Sunshine Coast." In my heart, I think she would have said the Gold Coast if Kylie and I hadn't gone there a few weeks earlier. I'd never been to the Sunshine Coast, so why not?

Kylie and Jo had ordered different wines with their lunch, and they both sipped at their drinks. Kylie asked Jo how hers was, and they had a little chat about each of the varieties and ended up taking a sip of each other's, then comparing notes again. I checked the mirror a second time.

When the waiter brought our meals, they asked if Grace would like a kiddie pack. It had a colouring page, some pencils and a couple of games, apparently. They had Grace at "colouring," and she studiously spent the next half hour staying firmly inside the lines.

I'd called the waiter, "They," because I'd had a lecture from Kylie about assuming people's gender. Social media was all over that, it seemed, and the whole concept of gender appeared to be a hot topic with Kylie anyway, perhaps because her People had been genderless. I agreed to do better, but I couldn't stop using a female pronoun with her. I'd just got too used to it.

The thaw in Jo had to be seen to be believed. Had Kylie cast a spell on her? It wouldn't surprise me. How could it?

She'd been some kind of wisp in the water six weeks ago and could bend water and air to her will. Why wouldn't she know a few spells? To be honest, I was surprised she hadn't yet found a cure for cancer, fixed the environment, and engineered world peace. Instead, she blamed humans for... well, everything, basically, and tried to get me to give up eating animal products. I pointed out that a woman happy to eat aloo gobi morning, noon, and night was hardly the poster child for veganism, but I capitulated somewhat and tried to eat less meat than I used to.

After we'd dropped Jo and Grace off with accompanying hugs, kisses, and an agreement to talk soon about the holiday, Kylie and I set off up Benjamin Way. I had to know whether she'd used some kind of magic. "What just happened? Where did all her anger go? How come you and her are such great mates now?"

She tittered. "I did what I promised I wouldn't do to you. I felt what she felt. She's mad at you. What is it you say? She's as mad as a cut spider."

"Snake. Cut snake."

"She's mad at Steve too. He works too much and leaves her to take care of Grace. You know, she said all this. Don't you listen to anything she says?"

"I didn't hear her say any of that."

"She didn't use those words, silly. You have to listen to what she's telling you, not what words she's saying. I don't think you're very good at that."

"Well pardon me for not being the Lady Of The Lake with ESP and sixth sight." Yep, I was a bit put out.

"I didn't mean you particularly. You, the humans."

"I get the business about Steve. I have heard her say that a bit, I suppose. How did you get her to warm to you? I swear she would have shot you when she saw you through the door if she'd had a gun and a psychotic personality."

"It's hard to dislike someone who likes you and is on your side, full of empathy."

I shook my head. "You couldn't have strung a sentence together if it hadn't been for my dictionary. I'm not sure I'm ready for you to take over as her bloody mother."

I didn't like the silence. It was one of those silences that says something unpleasant is coming, but the person who's about to do or say it is trying to think of a way to sweeten the pill. "Can I be honest?"

"Always." I had to say that. I had to believe the orgasms hadn't been fake.

"I think you love Jo, but I'm not sure you like her."

"I've told you she's hard work. She was always a handful."

"You've told me she thinks you didn't care for her as a child. Maybe that was only her perception, but what have you done to change her mind, other than argue with her about it?"

I squirmed a bit in my seat. It wasn't uncomfortable, but I was. I muttered, miserable. "When do you go back into that bloody lake?"

"She's not hard work." I noticed she'd avoided the question. "She's hard to understand, but I think you all are. Once you understand her, she's a pussy cat. Shall we get a cat, by the way?"

"I'm allergic."

"Bullshit."

I glanced at her. She was smiling. "I'm not in love with your new-found tendency to swear so much. I'm not a cat person."

"Have you ever had a cat?"

"No."

"How do you know you aren't a cat person, then? Six weeks ago, you weren't attracted to women."

I pulled into the drive, grateful we'd reached the house, and I could escape the torture of the conversation. "I'll think about it. And I'll try to do better with Jo."

"Good answers. I might need a lie down."

"Must be all that armchair philosophising you've been doing. Need to recover your energy?"

She leaned over and kissed me. "No. I need to use it up."

34

The Sunshine Coast was a great success. I rented a big house that meant we could socialise but also have our own space whenever we needed a break. Kylie had been right about Grace; her first visit to a beach reminded me of Kylie's, and the two of them spent hours in the water together while the rest of us watched from the sand. I worried it would further cement Grace's belief that Kylie was a mermaid, but they hit if off so well, I couldn't bring myself to suggest Kylie spend less time in the sea with her.

Steve seemed restless for the first couple of days, but in the end, I think it had been what he needed; an excuse to down tools and spend more time with his family. The tension between him and Jo eased, and one night at dinner, he even did an interesting thing. I can't remember what it was, but it made me laugh at the time.

The flights were a bit of a drag. No airlines flew non-stop from Canberra, so we had to go via Sydney, which involved an early morning flight out. Air travel hadn't recovered from the effects of COVID, and the fares were expensive, but what the hell? If it helped heal our strange little family, it was worth it.

At one point, Steve or Jo mentioned Fiji, but I steered the conversation away from anything that required Kylie to prove who she was. At every turn, something like that would come up, some innocent snippet of conversation or something I'd see on the television or on my iPad, and I'd be struck by the difficulty of the relationship I'd become so committed to. Kylie had no citizenship of any nation. We couldn't prove who she was; even her name had been invented.

Such thoughts invariably led me, morose and frightened, to think about her task. At some point, we had to face the inevitable moment when she would go into the lake, do whatever it was she had to do, and we would learn whether she could come out again. I wanted to put it off for ever; I wanted to do it right away. The longer we left it, the more time I had with her; the sooner we did it, the more time we'd have together without that sword of Damocles hanging over us, assuming she came out again.

After four days, Jo and I were alone on the beach. Steve had gone off to look for a toilet, and Kylie and Grace splashed in the water, which they did every day. I decided it would be a good time to ask a question that had burned in my mind all week. "How come you and Kylie are so friendly now, after all the things you said at your place that night?"

She didn't answer for a while, and I checked to see she hadn't fallen asleep. She stared up at the uninterrupted blue canvas above us and lay as still as a corpse. At last, she replied. "I was wrong about her. I'd had too much to drink. She's a decent person. Too good for you."

There she was. I'd begun to think we'd left Jo behind and brought a doppelgänger instead, with its chip set to "Happy."

"Thank you darling. I love you too. What changed your mind?"

"Grace. She's three and doesn't trust anybody as far as she could spit a rat."

"Nice analogy." I shivered at the thought.

"She took to the mermaid from the start, and she's never done that with anyone. She talks about her all the time, you know. It drives me batshit crazy. 'When is Kylie coming again?' 'Can we see Kylie and Grannie this week?'"

"Wait, Kylie and Grannie, or the other way round?"

"I said what I said." I'm fairly sure she sniggered at that, but I let it slide, and she went on. "Whenever I thought about her, she'd always been nice, even though I hadn't always been very nice to her." Kylie had sworn at Jo that night at dinner, but I didn't remind her. If she'd been too drunk to remember, it served her right. "When she suggested the holiday, it made so much sense. It was as though she could read my mind. Are you okay, Mum?"

I'd taken a sip of water right before she said that, and her words sent it down the wrong hole. I spluttered, coughed, and nodded my head in reassurance. "*If you only knew.*"

"The more I see of her, the more I like her. I was wrong. She's cool."

I raised my head and watched Kylie splashing around with Grace. Their raucous laughter filled the air with happiness and made the sun chuckle along, and I smiled. "She is cool."

"Too good for you."

I swiped a hand at her. "Jealousy will get you nowhere."

We didn't say any more about it. Nothing needed to be said. Kylie had won Jo over, just like she'd said, just like she'd done with me. Kylie was special, and I'd just got lucky that day I'd sat on that bench with my coffee.

We'd been back from the holiday a week, three months after she first came out of Lake Ginninderra, when she suggested we discuss her task and come to a decision. I'd dreaded the moment, hadn't had the courage to raise it myself even though I worried about it almost every day.

I tried to put it off. I came up with every excuse I could think of to procrastinate. I feigned toothaches, headaches, belly-aches, kneeaches, you name it. I looked through the baseball schedule and pointed out all the big games coming up for her team. She'd asked for a subscription to some baseball streaming service that meant she could watch Seattle whenever she wanted, and I'd been happy to get it for her. It brought her so much joy, even when Seattle appeared to play so bad she swore at the television and said they weren't worth watching. The next day, she'd be back in front of the television, cheering them on as they made up for the day before or compounded her misery by losing back-to-back games.

One night, Seattle had what she called an off-day, and she took my book out of my hand and said we couldn't avoid it anymore. I suggested we could avoid it for as long as we wanted, and I broke down into tears at the prospect of discussing it any further. She held me close, whispered soothing words, kissed me, and ran her fingers through my hair, but she insisted on the conversation.

I sniffed. "You start."

"There's nothing to discuss, really. We both know I have to do it. The Guardians will probably already be furious with me over how long I've taken."

"It's only been three months."

"It has, and I doubt I could ever spend such a happy three months again, but I can't ignore my responsibility. I'm not residing in the Balance while I'm here with you, because I'm ignoring my task to re-populate the new water with my People."

More sniffing. It's a gross thing, really, but I couldn't help it. My tears were tripping me. "You can't be as happy with me in future as you are now?"

"That's not what I meant. I want to spend forever with you, but I have a task to perform, and it's time to face it."

I dragged the back of a hand across my eyes. "Kylie, I've waited my whole life for you, but I didn't realise it until I found you. What if you can't come back?"

Kylie didn't answer, other than the tear that slid from an eye and trickled down her cheek. What could she say? She knew how it would affect me. The only thing she didn't know was how it would affect her. She might not remember me, or she might remember me and not be able to come out. She could swim around near the shore and look at me all she liked, but if she couldn't get out again, we couldn't be together.

I didn't give up, but sometimes there's only one choice, even if it's no choice at all. "When?" The small word in a small voice carried all our hopes and fears in it.

"Soon. At the weekend, maybe. The sooner we do it, the sooner we can get back to our life together."

My voice almost broke as I croaked out the word she hadn't said. "Perhaps."

"Winona seemed confident."

"She said a lot of stuff, and I don't think you really believed much of it at all."

She wiped at a tear as it trickled from her eye down her cheek. "That doesn't make her wrong."

35

The conversation had left me devastated, and when she proposed this weekend, my heart died in my breast. So soon. So little time. I had to hide behind something. I couldn't let her see how broken she had left me. "You'd better come back out, or I'll come in and find you."

She laughed a teary laugh. "When I come back out, can we get a cat?"

I'd never had a cat. Australia is dog country, not that I'm crazy about dogs either. Cats get a bad rap here because they kill native animals. So do we, with our bloody cars, all the time, but nobody ever suggested we should be licensed, neutered, and forced to live indoors. "If you promise to come out, we'll get a cat." I could live with it if I had Kylie, probably.

"Deal." Her smile jump-started my heart, which is probably a good thing. The alternative wasn't pretty. "She has to be a rescue cat though."

"She?"

"Of course. A tabby, if we can find one. They're so cute."

I got the feeling I might regret the decision to get this bloody feline. Kylie seemed as though she would be a sook about it, but as long as she emptied its litter box, that could be an advantage; I could see that. "I get to pick its name then."

"Done.

We went to bed. I didn't have much time left to enjoy her, and I didn't want to waste it talking about bloody cats.

Kylie seemed to feel the same, and she didn't watch much baseball that week. We went for a walk up Mount Painter again, a repeat of the first walk we'd taken together. The time had gone so quickly, and that first walk seemed like a dim memory now. How much my life had changed in those three months or so. A stiff breeze ruffled our hair, and we laughed at the thought it might be Winona teasing us.

The days refused to drag, and Friday night arrived far sooner than I felt ready for. Jo rang for a chat. Our differences seemed resolved, and I assumed the argument had been little more than a drunken outburst. It had been nasty, personal, and vindictive, but things like that happen between mother and daughter, I presumed. I couldn't remember such arguments with my own mother, who I rarely spoke to anymore. She had left my dad while I was in my teens and moved somewhere in northern Queensland. My dad had never been the same again and had died too young five years ago. I blamed mum, who had never told me why she left us behind. There might have been another man, but on the rare occasions we spoke—Christmas, birthdays—she never mentioned any significant other. Perhaps she had jumped teams as well. That would be hilarious, in a tragic sort of way.

My siblings and I weren't close either. My sister, Ellen,

lived in New York, so we'd lost touch a bit. We still FaceTimed now and then, but it was infrequent, and I hadn't talked to her since before Kylie came on the scene. I didn't know what she'd make of me coming out as gay, or bi, or whatever I was. She was younger than me and had always been a bit religious. She married an American, and he was a very serious man indeed. He made Rick look frivolous. He had a deep faith, as many Americans do, and I'm sure he would have some choice quotes from Leviticus for my new lifestyle.

My brother had been a wild child from my earliest memories. Two years older than me, I think he'd been dropped into a box of angry when he'd been a baby and swallowed more of it than was healthy. He'd spent time in prison, had more than one run-in with drugs and alcohol addiction, and once Jo came along, the devout middle class mum in me told me not to let him anywhere near my daughter. He'd ring every now and then to try to wheedle money out of Mike and me, but he hadn't rung for years. He didn't even know Mike had been killed. I imagined he'd been locked up for life or something. Best thing, perhaps.

I didn't tell Jo about Kylie going away, and I think I kept it quiet because I didn't want to admit there could be a chance I'd never see her again. Of course, if I said Kylie was leaving, and she was there next time I went to Jo's, that would lead to more awkward questions, and right now, I didn't have the strength to even contemplate such an outcome.

In bed that night, Kylie and I chatted about the timing of our trip to Lake George. It would be tomorrow morning. Our last night together, maybe. I cried so much, I couldn't understand where the tears came from. The human body is about sixty percent water, and six months ago, I'd found a calculator online that suggested I had about thirty-four litres of water in me. It's a little-known fact that there is water in our teeth, and I reckon the little bit in my teeth must have been all that remained that night after I cried myself to sleep on my wet pillow.

During the night, I must have sleep-cried that last bit of water out of my teeth. My mouth was drier than the Sahara Desert in a drought, and my tongue had glued itself to the top of my mouth. I dragged myself out to the kitchen for a glass of water. As usual, Kylie had already got up and sat on the lounge. I carried my glass of water over and sat beside her. She rested her head on my shoulder, and my body found a small oasis somewhere deep in my bones or something that it drained to support fresh tears.

I didn't know much about the Lake George area, but there are a couple of rest stops on the Federal Highway next to the lake. I presumed I would park there, and we would walk somewhere secluded so Kylie could take her clothes off and dive in.

She looked bashful. "I don't want everyone to see me naked." *How human of her.* "Couldn't I just dive in fully clothed?"

"I suppose you could, but when you come back, you'll have to put sopping wet clothes on."

"I don't mind." She tried for a half-hearted smile, but I didn't have enough fragments left to piece together even half of my heart.

Humour is often a good way to hide pain, and I had nothing else to shelter behind now the morning had arrived. "I do. You're not dripping Lake George all over the inside of my car. You'll just have to toughen up and flash those titties."

"I'll do it for you. I'd do pretty much anything for you, I

think." She smiled again, a better effort this time. Seven out of ten from the Cook judge.

I tried one last time. "There is one thing you could do for me, then. Don't go. Stay here. There's bound to be another drought soon enough, and the lake will dry up again. Have you thought about that? You might die."

"We call it fade. I would fade."

A snippet from a song came into my head, something about love and not fading away, but I couldn't remember what the song had been called. "I don't care what you call it. Don't go. Please."

"Have you never made a promise you felt compelled to keep?"

I sniffed. "My wedding vows, I suppose. Not that Mike bothered..."

I had never told her about Mike's affair, and I hoped she'd miss the small reference to it, but her mind was as sharp as one of those kitchen knives they show on the television, where they cut up shoes and cans with it. I mean, who needs to cut up their shoes with a kitchen knife?

"What's for dinner, mum?"

"Training shoe Bolognese with shoelaces spaghetti."

"Yum. My favourite."

I digress. Kylie looked deep into my eyes. "Mike didn't bother to... what?"

With a dejected sigh, I decided to tell her. It would give us more time together at least. "He had an affair. Jo would have been about seven or eight. I'd gained a lot of weight while I was pregnant, and I didn't try hard to lose it afterwards. Over the years, I put on more, and he started to make little comments about it, about how I wasn't the woman he'd married. I took it all in my stride, said I would take up running or working out, but I never did."

Kylie took my hand in hers. "Why did he say such horrible things?"

I wiped at my eyes. "You'd have to ask him that, baby. Only you can't, because he's dead. Anyway, there was this woman at work, one of the admins. Slim, good-looking, great hair. Not as great as yours, of course." I ran my other hand through Kylie's hair. "They started an affair. When I finally caught him, he said it had been going on for about a year."

"How did you catch him?"

I cry-laughed. "They were here. In our bed. I'd gone out for a night in town with Lucille, but she got crook and called it off. I was already on the bus, so I had to get off, come home again. And they were here. He was screwing her in my bloody bed."

"Ouch. That must have been tough."

"It was for him. I kicked him in the balls."

Kylie threw her head back and guffawed. "Double ouch. Did you hit her?"

"She was younger than me and went to the gym a lot. She had these biceps she always showed off in short sleeves. I didn't want to chance a fight with her. She'd have kicked my arse."

We both laughed, genuine amusement rather than crying and laughing at the same time. "My money would still have been on you."

"Why, thank you dear, but you should have seen those biceps."

"What happened?"

"He stopped seeing her. We talked round and round for so long, it drove me crazy. Jo needed us both, so we stayed together. He promised to end the affair, I promised to get in shape, and we made it work."

"Did you still love him?"

"Of course. Love can't be switched on or off like a light bulb. He'd been a bastard, but I still loved him." I hesitated. "Not like I love you, but I loved him."

"I wish I could understand this love emotion. It sounds wonderful."

I snorted snot onto her track suit pants, but I wiped it up with a tissue. "Love is the greatest pain in the arse ever, and the most wonderful thing it's possible to feel at the same time. You give your heart and just have to trust it doesn't get handed back to you all mangled up like a melon that's been run over by a B-Double."

She couldn't disguise the sadness in her smile, in her eyes. "I'm sorry you went through all that. I promise I'll never do the shagging with anybody but you when I come back."

"*If* you come back."

"When. Let's have some brekkie."

"You'd rather have brekkie than do the shagging?"

She shrugged. "Why does it have to be an either/or situation?"

36

We left a little after two. Kylie wanted to leave later so it would be twilight before she had to take her clothes off beside the lake, but I didn't want to be faced with the drive home, lonely and heartbroken, in the dark if she didn't come out. I don't like driving in the dark, and I didn't know how I could face the drive back if I had to make it alone, regardless of the time. I tried not to think about it, but the mind is a funny thing. The more you try not to think the worst, the more it plays over and over in your head, taunts you with the direst possible version of everything that might happen.

We were about halfway there when Rick rang. Honestly, you wouldn't read about it. Rick, Mr Nevergiveup. I couldn't face him, so I pressed the reject button on the steering wheel. One of these days, I must read the manual and work out how not to answer a call you're trying to reject. His voice turned down the music we'd been listening to. "Abi?"

"I'm in the car, Rick. Can I call you back later?"

"You're not holding your phone, are you?"

"*Piss off, man.*" "No, Rick, I'm not holding my bloody phone. I'm on hands-free."

"Good. That's illegal."

"Shit. Is it? Thank Christ you told me. I might have got a ticket otherwise."

I think it was a confused silence. "You said you weren't holding it."

"I lied. I'd better hang up quick, or this cop behind me might pull me over. I'll call you later." I wouldn't. "Bye Rick."

I laughed and turned to Kylie. "Oh my god. What a prawn."

"Abi, are you still there?"

Bugger. I hadn't disconnected. "Sorry Rick, the cop is pulling me over. Speak later."

I gestured for Kylie to disconnect the call, and she pushed at the screen in the middle of the dash. I didn't want to embarrass myself again. "Rick?"

Nothing. He'd gone. We laughed for a good two kilometres, which took us even closer to the lake. I usually love the moment when I come over the top of the rise and see the water ahead of and below me, but today I dreaded it. It couldn't be avoided unless I turned round or drove under a truck, and sure enough, I topped the rise and there it was, the reason Kylie existed. Without Lake George, I wouldn't have even known her, couldn't have enjoyed these months of happiness and joy, to say nothing of the best sex of my life. Now it stretched out in front of me, as if it laughed at me.

Everything that lake had given me, it was poised to take back, to claim for its own and rob me of the first person I'd ever loved without question. She'd brought me laughter, tears, joy, misery. She'd brought her weird friend who wasn't really a friend and who flew off into the night to haunt the phantoms in the sky she looked after. Kylie had been company, confessor, lover, and friend. Hell, I even ate less meat these days.

The road turned left, and so did we, although it occurred to me I could smash through the safety barrier and drive into the lake in a *Thelma and Louise* moment. Only one of us would die, though, and the lake would have won. I steeled my resolve; I'd beat that bloody lake, see if I didn't. I'd give up the love of my life to it, but I'd make sure it spat her back out to me. If it didn't, I'd buy every hair dryer in the city and evaporate the bloody thing. *"Don't mess with me, lake."*

I turned into the rest area and switched off the engine. There were more cars than I'd expected parked there next to the Federal Highway, people stretching legs, letting dogs pee, admiring the view of the lake and the wind turbines beyond. Kylie and I sat in the car for ten minutes in absolute silence. I couldn't think of anything to say that would help, and I imagined she couldn't either.

I sucked in a huge breath, turned and gave her a long, passionate kiss, then opened my door. I stood next to the car and stared over the shallow water of the lake. Two years ago, it had been fields where cows grazed, the occasional glint of sunlight from some small pocket of water way over on the Tarago side. After the fires, the rain had started, and it forgot to stop. As a result, we had our lake back, and now it wanted my hopes, my dreams, my happiness, my heart. My love.

I put my arm around Kylie's waist, she draped an arm around my shoulders, and we climbed the low fence. Somebody shouted something, but I didn't pay him any attention. He mightn't have shouted it at us. Maybe his kid had run out into the traffic, maybe his dog had shit on his shoes. I neither knew nor cared. The only thing that mattered was whether Kylie came back out of the water. Everything else could look after itself until that moment.

The ground was soggy as we turned towards some bushes on the northern side of the car park. If we passed them, they would offer Kylie a modicum of privacy, inadequate, but better than nothing. We splodged through the ground. Kylie had left her shoes in the car, but I hadn't been that smart, and they were already filthy.

We stopped, and so did my heart. How could it keep beating if she didn't come back? Why would I even want it to? A chill wind from the lake blew into our faces, and it felt like icy shards of despair and forlorn, fragile dreams. Kylie turned to look at me, and I placed a tender kiss on her lips. She glanced around, furtive, checking who could see her, I guessed, then slipped her sweatshirt over her head, pulled her track pants down, and kissed me again.

She dived in.

37

The water must have been all of fifteen centimetres deep where we were, but Kylie dived like one of the high divers in the Olympics. Most people would have broken their nose on some piece of rubbish lying just beneath the surface, or face-planted with a splurge of mud, but not Kylie. She disappeared. I'd seen her appear, so I should have been ready, but I wasn't. I took an involuntary step back, shocked, and looked around to see whether anybody had noticed. Nobody stared my way, so I guessed I was the only one to see it. There was no splash, not even a ripple.

I stood there for a while, anxious and jittery. I had no idea how long it might take her to do whatever she needed to, and maybe five minutes after she dived in, I stooped to pick up her discarded clothes. I waited, then waited some more. Nothing. The hole in my chest grew bigger and heavier. If I'd breathed, I hadn't realised it. I must have, but nothing registered other than the pain that tore my insides apart as I stared at the water and willed Kylie to come out of it.

It was cold standing there, and I wished I'd worn my puffer jacket. I stamped my feet, but that only splashed mud everywhere. Above me, dark, brooding clouds threatened rain, and the petrichor smell filled the air even though no rain had yet fallen. I wondered whether rain was Winona's thing or Kylie's. Could Kylie stop me getting wet if it started to rain while I waited for her? *"The things we do for love."* As I thought that, that bloody song by 10CC started playing in my head. Ear worm much?

I glanced at my watch. Quarter to four, nine degrees, no unread texts, six of twelve standing hours. It looked like I wouldn't close my activity rings today; too little exercise and too long sitting around in a miserable funk at home this morning. If she waited much longer, I might have to drive back in the dark, especially with those clouds. I don't like to drive in the dark. I say "drive," but the car had automatic headlight dipping, cruise control, lane assistance to make sure you stayed inside the lines, automatic transmission, and collision detection systems. I had to be in it, but beyond that, I had virtually nothing to do.

My watch told me almost everything, and my phone told me everything the watch didn't know. My car drove itself. With a few words from me, the television would change channels, turn itself up or down, switch to playing music, even turn itself off. I'd become redundant in my own life, and if Kylie didn't come out of the lake, that looked like a bleak proposition at that moment.

A bucket-worth of water splashed up out of the lake in my direction. Most people would have run, screaming in terror, but

I smiled. Kylie. She could see me, at least. If she didn't emerge from the lake, maybe I could come out here from time to time so she could soak me. There would be some tiny piece of her in the droplets of water that dripped from me, which might be some consolation. I cried more tears than the water she had splashed at me, and still she didn't appear.

How long should I stand there, waiting, hoping against hope? I'd brought a big tote, and I pushed her clothes into it, then pulled them out again. If I left them in the bag, it might suggest I'd given up, and if she was watching, that might make her sad. I thought I could remember her saying they couldn't feel anything when they were in the water, no emotions of any kind, but I didn't want to take any chances that I might upset her.

What if she came out, but she looked different? What if fate decided to test me and make her look plain, overweight, and short, like me? I wouldn't care; I just wanted her to come out of the water and repair all the internal damage I'd suffered since she decided to fulfil her task.

I chewed at my bottom lip, nervous, and the dread in my chest intensified to an icy grip that squeezed my heart, tugged at my stomach. It had been fifteen minutes at least, and she hadn't reappeared. I glanced at the car park, where a man stared over at me. If I could see him, he could see Kylie if she came out. Maybe she was waiting for some privacy. *"He must wonder what I'm up to."* It was none of his damn business, and I took an aggressive step towards him.

He turned away, and I heard water splash behind me. I wheeled, afraid Kylie had done nothing more than flick more water at me, but there she was, her long, blonde hair plastered to her head and down past her shoulders. Figure still sickeningly awesome. Water flowed from her long, slender fingers and drew a pair of wet lines in the grass as she took a hesitant step towards me.

The moment had arrived. Kylie had returned, but I froze, unable to move as the cold dread gave way to a joy that bounced around in my chest, ricocheted off my ribs, side to side like that old tennis game we used to play on the television before video games became more life-like than life itself. I forced words out of me on a tortured breath. "Hello, you."

"Hello, you."

She smiled and reached for me, and my inertia broke. I ran two steps into her arms, almost bowling her over. "You're back." That was obvious, of course, but I was lost for words at that moment.

"Back."

I knitted my brows. It seemed she had forgotten how to speak English, but I'd been prepared for that. I ratted around in the bottom of my tote, pulled out my dictionary, and handed it to her. She stared at it, opened it to the first page, then laughed. "I'm just teasing. I haven't forgotten the language. I'm impressed you brought this though." She waved the dictionary in the air like she had in my lounge room that first day.

I glanced back to the car park. Old mate was staring again, harder this time. I thrust Kylie's clothes at her. "Get dressed, you idiot. There's someone perving on you from the car park."

We swapped the clothes for the dictionary, and I shoved the book back into my tote. Kylie looked up once she'd dressed herself. "Do I look the same?"

I swept my eyes up and down her. Same irritatingly perfect figure, same smile. "Your hair's wetter than the first time, but other than that, yes. You're Kylie. Welcome back." We embraced, and I cried unashamed, happy tears. "What took you so long? You drove me crazy. I thought you weren't coming back."

"Our time isn't the same as yours. I divided, and my division chose a name. It's a very important ceremony among our People, and I didn't want to abandon them as they chose their name. Besides, I had to confirm with the Guardians the name had never been taken before, which it hadn't. The Guardians were not happy with me. I had taken too long, they said."

"What do they know? You didn't take long at all, and anyway, you're back now, and I'm never letting you go in like that again. It broke my heart."

"I'm sorry, but it was important. The lake will be fine now. My division can divide until there are enough People for the water and animals. Because the Guardians told me I wouldn't be able to come back out, I was afraid. I saw you, and I wanted to come out, but I was scared to try, in case I found myself trapped. It would have broken my heart as well. I didn't feel ready for that pain. When you turned away from the lake, I thought you'd given up, thought you'd decided to go home. I couldn't stand the agony, so I willed myself to come out."

I pulled a confused face. "I thought you couldn't feel in that form."

She kissed the end of my nose. "I'm back, and we have a big decision to make."

I nuzzled her neck. "No decisions. I want to get you home and into bed."

Kylie held me at arm's length. "You can't avoid this decision, and I want us to make it before we leave."

I sighed, exasperated. "Okay, okay. What is this mighty decision?"

Her grin teased me, but it drove away the rainclouds from my heart too. "What will we call the cat?"

I gasped in irritation, then a thought occurred to me, and I smiled and forced my way back into her embrace. On tiptoes, I whispered into her ear. "Dannii."

She laughed once, and stroked the back of my head, then stopped. "Wait a minute. Isn't there a Kylie Minogue who has a sister—"

She'd worked it out, and I interrupted her. "There is, and the best part is it will drive Jo bloody crazy."

Kylie kissed the top of my head. "Dannii it is, then."

"Come on then, let's—"

It was her turn to interrupt. "Wait a moment. There's something else I have to talk about." I opened my mouth and drew in a breath, but she pressed a finger against my lips to stop me. "When I flitted around nearby and watched you, you looked so frightened, so desperate, so miserable. It hurt me."

"It hurt me too."

Her finger muffled my words a little, and she clamped a hand over my mouth. "Let me finish, please. It hurt me, Abi. I'm not supposed to be able to feel pain in my natural form. We don't feel anything: warm, cold, happy, sad, tired, refreshed. I did, though. I felt pain, and as I watched you, I realised something else."

I reached up and pulled her hand away from my mouth. "What?"

"I'd been saying all along I couldn't understand the feelings you had for me, that it was unnatural to me. As I watched you here on the bank, waiting, hoping, longing, I realised I could understand it. I realised I love you."

I think I might have collapsed if she hadn't had her arms

around me. My head swam, dizziness turned my legs to jelly, my blood roared in my ears. Had I heard her right? Had she just said she loved me? "Say that again."

"I love you."

I buried my head in her stupendous bosom and wept, unashamed. This magnificent person, the gentlest, kindest person I'd ever met, other than that one time at Jo's, for which plenty of excuses could be made, loved me? What had I done to deserve this sort of luck? I looked up at her, tears blurring my vision. "I love you too. Those minutes you were gone lasted years. They ground my heart, my soul, my bones to dust, scattered them on the wind. Nothing could repair me except you. And you came back."

"That I did." She took my hand and turned me towards the car park. Old mate still stared at us. He'd have quite a tale to tell everyone in the pub tonight, but nobody would believe a bloody word of it.

I rubbed the side of my head against Kylie's arm. "Let's go home."

SOME OF THE AUSSIE/NZ TERMS EXPLAINED

Belco

Short for Belconnen, a suburb of Canberra

Puffer jacket

Quilted jacket

Commodore

A popular type of car manufactured by Holden (GM)

Unit

Apartment

The Seekers

A folk/pop group from the sixties and seventies

Pissed

Drunk

Crook

Sick

Last wicket stand

A cricket term meaning the last two batsmen remaining

Grog

Alcohol

Dob, Dobbed

Report to authorities

I'll be right

I'll be fine

Trackie dacks

Track or sweat pants

Tiki touring

(NZ) General touring around, on holiday etc

Wanker

Unpleasant person

Toastie

Toasted sandwich

but (at the end of a sentence)

Used instead of though

Firies

Firefighters

CPA

Certified Public Accountant

B-Double

Large truck with two semi trailers attached

Shoey

Skull a drink, usually champagne, from a shoe

FOGO

Food organics and garden organics - a service that collects green waste

Eat the arse out of a low-flying duck

Really hungry

Block-out

Suntan lotion

Sook

Timid, a crybaby

Plumber's smile

The bottoms of the buttocks, often seen when someone wears very short shorts

ACKNOWLEDGMENTS

Cover by David at David Schembri Studios (davidschembristudios.com)

Email David at dschembristudios@gmail.com

Taylor at Origami Graphics (https://origamigraphics.net.au), who created the Hayley Price Books logo, many other graphical logos and banners, and brought my website up to date.›

Paperback copies of this book bought direct from me are printed in Australia by Instant Colour Press, Belconnen (https://instantcolourpress.com.au/), who also print my bookmarks and character art. Please support local independent businesses.

SPECIAL THANKS

Ailsa. Without you, there could have been none of this whirl-wind ride. I'm so happy I got to take it with you.

Members of the emergency services across Australia

Your selfless devotion to duty keeps us all safe, every day. You don't do it for the thanks, but we appreciate you and thank you from the bottoms of our hearts.

ABOUT THE AUTHOR

KASSIE ANDERS is a pen name of Hayley Price. Hayley has always been a storyteller. Throughout her life, she has told her story through songs as the principal songwriter in several bands, most recently Adventures With Alice, whose songs feature in many of her books.

A New Zealander, Hayley currently lives in Canberra, Australia, with her long-time partner and a grumpy, bossy cat called Rosie. She loves baseball and suffers eternal torture as a fan of the San Francisco Giants. Music has been a major part of her life, and outside her own compositions, she is an enormous fan of Christopher Cross as well as Daryl Hall & John Oates and underrated 80s UK prog-rock band Voyager, who once named her their #1 fan.

Books written under Kassie's pen name will tend to be more romance-oriented, and more light-hearted in nature than most of Hayley's other work.

LINKS

Here are some links I hope you will find useful.

My website: https://hayleyprice.net

Please leave a review for this book. Find a link at bio.site/hayleyprice

Why not sign up for my monthly newsletter, filled with information and special offers? www.hayleyprice.net/#newsletter